T0089495

NUMBER
87

Eden Phillpotts as Harrington Hext

PROLOGUE BOOKS

F+W Media, Inc.

Published by
PROLOGUE BOOKS
an imprint of F+W Media, Inc.
10151 Carver Road, Suite 200, Blue Ash, Ohio 45242
www.prologuebooks.com

ISBN 10: 1-4405-4474-3
ISBN 13: 978-1-4405-4474-3
eISBN 10: 1-4405-4473-5
eISBN 13: 978-1-4405-4473-6

Printed in the United States of America.

10 9 8 7 6 5 4 3 2 1

Introduction

The series of international events here to be chronicled in connection with that astounding apparition, known in the United Kingdom and the United States of America as "the Bat," while challenging and wakening the terror of the civilized world, yet possessed for one little, commonplace community a unique significance. That company was represented by the Club of Friends, and for this reason it is necessary that a glimpse of the club should open the narrative.

Fate, which is only another name for human temperament writ large, decreed that a figure second to none, even as it stands, in the history of civilization should never attain to its true dimensions, or win that acclaim its achievement deserved. Instead, human limitations leavened the lump of genius and he, who might have been one of the world's supreme figures, remains forever beneath the stature of lesser men than himself.

Temperament ruined all, and the following record not only chronicles a series of events contrary to human experience and unparalleled in human story, but relates, between the lines, a tragedy comparable to the Greek in its tremendous and solemn proportions. For once again Prometheus set foot upon earth in the likeness of a man, and once again a jealous fate tormented the Lightbringer and confounded his magnificent contribution to the world's hope of happiness. But no Zeus came between the hero of this awful narrative and his gift to humanity. A darker and subtler destiny was his: to be denied the fruit of his own lifelong devotion by inherent qualities of mind; and to be chained forever on the arid precipice of the world's hatred in gyves forged by himself.

Such confusion of attributes, such greatness and littleness within a single heart, cost civilization a treasure beyond human power to estimate, or indeed conceive. Providence, with one hand, offered the children of men such a boon and bounty as life has not known; and with the other drew it back again. Nor shall Providence be blamed when the tremendous tale is told and its implications perceived.

—E. G.

Contents

Chapter I

The Death of Alexander Skeat

The Club of Friends was an organism purely social. We met after the work of the day for relaxation and amusement; but certain rules and reservations served always to limit membership, and I think that at no time did we ever number more than five and twenty members. Yet the institution had attained a respectable age, and while most of the rising generation preferred conditions more entertaining and diversified, there never lacked men to enlist in the Club of Friends. When Chislehurst first became a popular suburb of London, a few early, private residents planned the community; and though they were now all gone, others had succeeded them.

I, for example, followed my father, and my friend, Leon Jacobs, had succeeded old Isidore Jacobs, the founder of the club.

We met in the evening and enjoyed conversation on all subjects of human interest; while, as an innovation, at the proposal of Bishop Blore, the present doyen of the club, we started a winter session of short lectures and invited eminent publicists to visit us, accept our hospitality and afterwards entertain us with brief addresses, or air their social opinions, followed by discussion. But the experiment was short lived. Few eminent men cared to be troubled, or could spare the time; while those minor celebrities who did accept our invitation, dine with us at their convenience, and afterwards propound their theories for human advancement, proved too biased, too possessed with the paramount importance of their own convictions on art, politics and economics, to attract unprejudiced listeners.

The last who came was a man of European reputation, and the tragedy and mystery that surrounded the end of Alexander Skeat followed within a week of his visit. His death created a deep impression in our little circle, and it seemed hard to believe that this famous figure, so full of vitality and the electric energy of genius, should, at the height of his fame, have vanished into the unknown without explanation.

At the close of our evening with Mr. Skeat—an evening marked by vigorous setting forth of irreconcilable doctrines—Jacobs and I had attended him to the railway station through the darkness of a winter night.

The great man warned us against sensuality and all indulgence, against indifference, coldness of heart, overmuch curiosity and every form of materialism and greed. He spoke of the iniquities of the middle class and prophesied their well-deserved extinction. He then turned upon one Paul Strossmayer, our latest and none too popular guest member, whose views he had furiously opposed. He swore that Strossmayer was a deep knave and in every respect an undesirable alien.

"I read faces as lesser men read books," he said, "and I read in this Jugo-Slav, or Serb, or Czecho-Slovake, or whatever he calls himself, a dangerous and anti-human impulse. Be warned and deny him your hospitality or friendship. Under that astute and suave exterior there hides a crafty, calculating, godless rascal with a heart of flint."

Skeat was soon gone and I must confess we breathed the easier for his departure. Returning to the club, we found opinion rather set against him and his fiery exegesis; for such is the British instinct, that his onslaught on Strossmayer inclined even those who did not like the new member to take his side.

A week later the murder of Alexander Skeat startled Europe and America.

I transcribe an account published in *The Times* on the morning after the tragedy.

"We regret to report the death of Mr. Alexander Skeat under extraordinary circumstances. As yet no light has been thrown upon his sudden end, but there can be little doubt that the famous author lost his life at the hand of an assassin, though the manner of the murder and the person of the murderer are as yet unknown.

"Returning last night from a lecture at the Eccentric Club, near the hour of midnight, Mr. Skeat was crossing St. James's Park, when death overtook him.

"A policeman, standing at the time on the suspension bridge that crosses the ornamental waters, heard a single, loud cry from the path that approaches the bridge easterly, and hastening to the spot he found a man lying upon his face on the grass at the path side. Close at hand, though but dimly visible, for the night was foggy, P.C. 849 declares that he saw a large and living animal, such as he had never seen before. He attempts no exact description of this creature, but has sworn that he distinguished a black, humped object, 'as large as a horse' with a very long neck and a narrow head above which were set tall ears. Its eyes shone like a cat's as he turned his lantern upon it, and it appeared to hesitate as he advanced a short distance towards it. He then blew his whistle, and the thing, evidently alarmed, hopped twice, then spread black wings, ascended swiftly into the air and disappeared. The constable likens the creature to a huge bird, and though four other officers, who ran to answer his summons, saw nothing of this alleged *rara avis*, in one particular they corroborate a detail reported by John Syme (P.C. 849). All were conscious of an overpowering taint and reek in the air—an animal smell. Herbert Adams—a constable from the country—described it as though he had 'run into a dozen foxes.' Subsequent examination, however, revealed no trace of any disturbance to turf or soil; but the area where Mr. Alexander Skeat perished has been railed off and guarded for more careful investigation today.

"The unfortunate gentleman appeared to be quite dead. He was carried to the St. James's Street police station and Dr. Forbes Weston, who arrived within ten minutes, recognized the victim and found life to be extinct.

"It is not too much to describe this sudden destruction of an extraordinary genius as an international disaster, for Alexander Skeat was still but fifty-four and his creative energy far short of exhaustion. We shall examine his achievement and its significance tomorrow; but for the moment can only chronicle an end upon which no ray of explanatory light has yet fallen.

"The theory of death at the onset of an unknown and savage animal in the heart of the metropolis appears too extravagant to be entertained and we prefer to believe that time will presently reveal a murder, though whether the purpose and the perpetrator of the crime are discovered remains to be seen. An autopsy takes place this morning."

The evening papers of that day conveyed particulars of the postmortem examination, and this increased the mystery of Skeat's end. For the result neither confirmed nor contradicted the opinion of *The Times.*

There was no wound upon the body of the dead man, and only chance determined the operators to investigate a small red speck discovered under Skeat's left shoulder-blade. It looked, as the newspapers said, like the bite of a flea or the prick of a pin. Here, however, at this almost imperceptible point, death had entered, and examination showed an incision no wider than a thread which persisted from the skin through the tissues to the heart. Therein it disappeared. There were no inflicted wounds of any sort, though a bruise on the forehead showed that Alexander Skeat had fallen forward and struck his head as he fell. But analysis, while it revealed no poison from this bite, or puncture, discovered a profound disturbance of the blood as a consequence of it—a disturbance believed at first akin to that which certain snake poisons are known to cause. The body of the dead man was also strangely affected. It revealed disintegration of its component parts and the introduction of an unknown material foreign to healthy bone and flesh. Chemists were conducting an examination on these problems.

The day brought no news from the police. Immense activity marked Scotland Yard and a wide net was spread for possible criminals. But upon no organization or society fell even suspicion. Skeat, while not openly willing to support the more unscrupulous of the organizations working against our Government and Constitution, in no sense could be said to have incurred their enmity. He was a fighter and a hard hitter; but if any regarded him as an adversary of law and order, they were those in authority: men of all least likely to commit lawless violence, or suppress an opponent by direct means. In England one may preach a wide measure of treason at will in books, newspapers and journals; it is only when we utter the same aloud at a street corner to a dozen loafers that we get locked up. This Skeat knew well enough and had always acted accordingly.

Enemies he possessed in plenty; but among them could be numbered no man likely thus to take the law into his own hands. Moreover the issue was confused by the few particulars recorded of his death. For it appeared certain that he had died under a force as yet a secret from science; and while the majority of those set to solve the problem discarded the theory of a savage and unknown poisonous animal, the fact remained that death had come through a channel absolutely unfamiliar to human experience.

Chapter II

The New Member

Before dealing with the new member it is necessary that some of the older supporters of the Club of Friends should first be mentioned.

General Fordyce and his younger brother, Sir Bruce, were bachelors both—indeed most of us belonged to that order. The general represented a typical reactionary mind, built on old traditions and a lifetime in the army; but his geniality, love of a jest, generosity and humanity made him far more popular than his brother—a much abler man, but lacking in charm, or social gifts. Yet Sir Bruce could claim quite as good a heart—upon that we all agreed. Both he and his brother had spent their working days in India. Sir Bruce was very learned, with a record of distinguished accomplishment behind him. For many years he had been Director of the Royal Botanical Gardens at Calcutta and had won the Fellowship of the Royal Society for his original work on the Chiroptera—the order of flying mammals, or bats. He had built himself a bungalow in the Eastern style at Chislehurst, while his elder brother dwelt not far off upon the Common in a modern villa. But Sir Bruce owned a second home in Devonshire—the family place, which General Fordyce lacked means to keep up and which he had, therefore, handed over to his brother. A great contrast was presented by the pair, for while the soldier loved his own voice and lightened his comments on men and things with invariable good humor, the man of science admitted himself a pessimist and seldom shared our hopes of amelioration for the race of man. Yet under his taciturn and watchful manner he was no cynic, and for my part, I always esteemed his reasoned opinions and valued any conclusions he might impart when in an amiable mood.

Bishop Walter Blore, a Colonial prelate now retired, preserved a mean between the brothers. He was conservative and a little suspicious of the world's progress in certain directions, but charity sweetened his outlook and enthusiastic religious faith kept his hope high.

One must also mention Jack Smith, a barrister who still practiced, though he was always talking of giving up, and Merrivale Medland, a wine merchant, a kind-hearted but credulous man, whom we respected and valued for his supervision of our modest cellar.

Of younger members there were not many. My friend, Leon Jacobs, was a stockbroker, and I, Ernest Granger, secretary of the Club of Friends, who now undertake this extraordinary narrative, pursued my business of actuary in the Apollo Life Assurance Society. Jacobs and I were of an age—thirty-five—and the infants of the club.

On the night when Paul Strossmayer first came amongst us, all those I have mentioned, save Bishop Blore, were present in the smoking room, and conversation, as usual, ran upon serious subjects.

Nature happened to be our theme and somebody—I think Jack Smith, whose hobby was rose-growing—declared that in Nature's categories mercy found no place.

"Neither passion nor compassion belongs to her," he said. "She never laughs, never relents and is as solemn and bloodthirsty and businesslike as a hunting owl."

Then Sir Bruce spoke. He was a little fellow and had a weak voice, which belied him, for few old Indians I have met enjoyed greater vigor of mind and body.

"Sentimental man and his pathetic fallacy have thrown dust into our eyes concerning Nature," he declared; "and so it comes about that we dignify her energies into something worthy of admiration, or disapproval, as the case may be. That is quite as futile as applauding a thousand horsepower steam engine for doing its work. Science has corrected this old attitude, or should do so. Science has revealed that what beauty, or horror, we may find in Nature's operations and phenomena lies in the human mind, which weighs these manifestations. We apply aesthetic tests to her outward appearance and control to her terrific energy. Thus we condemn her to the service of man and translate her into human values. In reality, she has no others."

"Probably that is why poets hate Science," I said; but General Fordyce protested.

"They cannot justly do so, for they must know that Science has improved the world out of knowledge, made it cleaner, sweeter, more wholesome, more adequate, more worthy of mankind. In a word, Science has helped to lift us above the brutes."

Sir Bruce spoke again from his armchair by the fire.

"There's another side to that. The poets remember what high explosives mean—and poison gas. Did those lift us above the brutes?"

"My dear Bruce, what a question! Emphatically they did; and who knows that better than you? If Science could help us to beat Germany by the only possible means left to do so, who shall reasonably blame her for the means?"

"Only the young poets, who, rather than fight, would have thrown open the door to Germany," said Jack Smith. "The youthful wiseacres, who avoided fighting, but have been so busy lecturing other people ever since the war ended. They despise Science, sublimely unaware that Science and Science alone kept the enemy's hoof off their own necks. Where would all these sleek canaries be if Germany had won?"

"Man may prostitute Science for his own selfish needs," I declared, "but that is her misfortune, not her fault."

Sir Bruce applauded my sentiment. "Well said, Granger," he answered.

Then Leon Jacobs spoke. He was a man of wide sympathies and acute intelligence.

"There's no doubt that a deep, common suspicion exists between the Arts and Science," he said. "We see it displayed, not only by the poets, but in the highest centers of learning. There is friction and what we call the 'humanities' in education are very jealous of Science—as though Science were not the most humane of all branches of human progress. Take the Carnegie Trust of two millions to the Scots Universities. Already in the administration of this immense sum Science, or those who represent her, find their sense of justice outraged by the steady transference of these endowments from themselves and what the testator intended, to more picturesque mental activities."

"Science is still the Cinderella," said Jack Smith; and at the same moment Mr. Paul Strossmayer entered the smoking room.

He was a man in the fullness of life—tall and spare, but with abundant physical and intellectual force. One had only to study his face to perceive qualities that lifted the expression out of the common. He was dark-skinned, with a close-cropped black beard and moustache, wonderful brown eyes, heavy, rather coarse hair, also close-cropped, and black eyebrows. His forehead was not high but distinguished by unusual breadth. It seemed to bulge out a little over his ears, which were set closely to his head and of great beauty. His nose was solid but well proportioned and his hands were an artist's—delicate, nervous and finely molded. The man, was, in fact, built to challenge and we found presently that he left none of us indifferent. Personally I always found something magnetic and attractive about him, and so did Leon Jacobs; but others he repelled from the first, and these never changed their opinion; though in the case of Medland, the wine merchant, and Jack Smith, they vacillated, sometimes professing to admire Strossmayer, then again detesting him. He spoke perfect English, with an accent and intonation very distinguished, and revealed great vivacity of movement. But his mannerisms were under restraint, and even in the heat of argument he was always courteous and agreeable. Indeed he showed deference to men older than himself, and while making no servile effort to ingratiate, preserved an urbane and amiable attitude to all. One felt curiously that he lived at higher pressure than we, with an intensity of feeling, conviction and ambition that were denied us. A patriotism almost passionate inspired him for his country, and he shared the hopes and dreams of a newborn nation. For he was a Jugo-Slav—a kinsman of that very famous Bishop Strossmayer, who, during his episcopate of five and fifty years, worked so nobly for the union of the Southern Slavs and a promised land which his eyes were not destined to behold. This good prelate had been known to Bishop Blore in past time, and it was our bishop who nominated the visitor, on hearing that he had become domiciled in England for the present with a family of his compatriots at Chislehurst.

Paul Strossmayer had been educated in England and now returned to it on specific service for the new State. He pursued his purposes with enthusiasm and made no secret of them. Indeed, upon the occasion of his first visit to the club, accident willed that he should give us particulars. General Fordyce made him welcome and he accepted our friendly reception with grace and even gratitude. He gave a first impression of an ambitious, self-centered man—a man who knew exactly what he wanted, was confident that he could achieve his purpose, and would not allow sentiment or any other emotion to come between him and his goal.

He ordered a whiskey and soda, drew a cigar from his case and went to one of the four writing desks that surrounded the smoking room. We then continued to pursue our subject and presently, when he had completed two letters, he changed his chair and occupied a vacant one beside me. He waited for a while, to pick up the gist of the topic, and when he had done so, revealed that our subject was not only interesting to him, but one upon which he stood deeply informed.

"You are touching the very matter that brings me to this country, gentlemen," he said pleasantly. "Permit that to be my introduction. Would you like me to speak?"

The ingenuous question attracted us.

"We were considering the application of Science to the great world problems of the future," I said.

"Surely the supreme, vital subject for all active minds," he answered. "Is there another topic remotely akin to this in gravity, or full of more tremendous significance? I hold a brief for Science. I, and those for whom I am privileged to work—the keenest intellects in Jugo-Slavia today—perceive with profound conviction that it is Science which will remold Europe and rebuild the second chaos, in which even our greatest statesmen now move as blind men. For in our judgment, the countries destined first to emerge from the confusion, the houses likely first to be set in order, are those which defer before all else to their chemist-philosophers. Yes, we link the terms, because through organic chemistry and its philosophical application shall emerge the supreme, physical powers to control and direct future civilization."

"A soulless hope," murmured General Fordyce.

"Sufficient for the day is the problem thereof," answered Paul Strossmayer.

"But would you set physical energies before the humanistic and spiritual power which others hold vital to rejuvenation of humanity?" asked Jack Smith. "Would you deny that to the Arts we must look first, and lead man upward from his heart rather than his head, Mr. Strossmayer?"

"We Jugo-Slavs are concerned with things as they are," he answered. "Humanity lives on its belly, and the soul of a hungry, angry, dishonored world can offer little material for human salvation, while its children lack food. We—first of all in the Balkans—are a spiritual nation, as I believe; but our eyes are wide open, as the eyes of long subjugated nations are apt to be. We labor under no delusions, or illusions, in the naked dawn light of our State, and we perceive that for a generation to come, civilization must be in the melting pot. The old security of the strong and the freedom of the mighty are gone. We are all in the same leaky boat, great and small together, and power is not vested in what you call 'the humanities'—far from it. Science, not the Arts, ended the war. War, indeed, is a ghost for a moment, but it remains for the men and women of this century to decide if the ghost shall vanish into thin air, or presently grow solid and clothe itself again with bones and flesh. We must, then, accept existing conditions and not indulge in metaphysics. Physics alone offers salvation. Physics alone is stronger than treaties and more trustworthy than the word of living man; because physics means power."

"You are a sad materialist, Mr. Strossmayer," said Merrivale Medland. But the other shook his head.

"The world is still under the tyranny of shibboleths," he answered, "and until our values can be stated in words, to be spoken and understood universally, there must lie a gulf of misunderstanding between the nations. No panacea will bridge this gulf, for diversity of languages must forever keep it open. Babel meant a deeper and more spiritual curse on progress than the most malignant interposition of the Devil. But let us turn to those languages that all speak with one tongue and understand with one heart, my friends. In the Arts, music is such a universal language; and chemistry in the Sciences. The men of Science labor under no such crushing disadvantage as our politicians, for in their search for truth, they recognize the hindrance of tongues and substitute symbols beyond possibility of two constructions. In Science, Jew and Gentile, East and West, Latin and Scandinavian, meet as upon sure ground."

He turned to Medland with his rather fascinating, sly smile.

"I am not a 'sad materialist,' but a convinced one—a joyous one—monsieur, though the word illustrates my argument very happily. Do you and I mean the same thing when we speak of 'materialism'? Assuredly not. If we all in this room set down on paper our understanding of that word's significance, would our definitions agree? Not two of them!

"Our purpose in Jugo-Slavia," he continued, "is simple and direct. We look ahead; we are aware that radioactivity is but the momentous discovery of yesterday; but we believe that, in the arcana of nature, exist forces beyond the dreams of mankind, and we are out, at this early stage in our corporate history, to discover and corner those forces if we can do so."

"'Corner' is a sinister word," said Jack Smith.

The other flinched a little.

"Hear me further," he replied. "How to discover and secure the unknown? Only by taking a line of action which, as yet, seems wholly foreign to the genius of the existing Great Powers. Not, of course, that all nations save your own, gentlemen, are not already busy on the great quest—they are; but success cannot be promised, because the seeker belongs to France, or England, Italy or the United States. It will probably come by chance, and in this tremendous hunt, the humblest of kingdoms—my own, is as likely to achieve success as the greatest. Indeed, more likely, for we are far more keenly alive to its significance and its possibilities than old empires, which have long known power and are, therefore, tempted to think on the old, conservative lines of what constituted power in the past."

General Fordyce regarded the speaker somewhat blankly.

"So that's what you little nations are after?" he asked.

"Why not, General? The little, new peoples acutely perceive their precarious foothold among the great, old peoples. They judge that, if the world is to be remolded along the old lines and the promises of peace made illusory, their liberty and independence are worthless words. We, at any rate, believe that the next war—if next there be—and nothing in the existing situation rules out the probability—we hold that the next war will not be one of numbers, but radioactivity; and realize that, upon such a basis, we have as good a chance as we might of the Old World, or the New. Consider one man: Hugo Stinnes, the German millionaire, at present engaged in getting a stranglehold on half the basic industries of the Continent. Suppose a chemist came to such a man and suggested that he might be upon the track of something more powerful than basic industries? Would Stinnes send the scientist about his business, as you sent those who first advocated the 'tank' in war? No; if a hundred young men approached him, he would find opportunity and encouragement for them all, because he would argue that, though ninety-nine were likely to fail, the hundredth might do the trick—win the paramount secret. That is the spirit that inspires all men and nations with foresight. Each hopes to be first—but England. Your country, glorious though she continues to be, has never possessed foresight. It is no part of your national endowment."

"You go too far, sir," said Medland somewhat warmly.

The Jugo-Slav bowed.

"I shall apologize if I am wrong," he answered. "But consider recent facts. None knows better than I in my present inquiries what encouragement original research receives here. I have heard it on a hundred tongues, gentlemen. Your men of science won the war: there is not a shadow of doubt about that. And you patted them on the back and gave the more fortunate trifling money presents and OBEs—and forgot them. The great rewards went to commanders on land and sea, not those who enabled them to win their victories. And now you have forgotten your scientists and, until you want them again, you will continue to forget them. But next time you will need mightier things than tanks, or Zeppelin destroyers, trinitrotoluene, or mustard gas.

"In the face of the hatred of the nations, we cannot rule out war. Germany hates the Poles, as all men hate those they have wronged; China hates Japan, as all men hate those who have wronged them. Hatred and distrust are rife, and the great peace did not lessen them by one smothered curse. We were on the high road to success, but the human ingredient intervened and reason went down. How, you ask? How was the opportunity lost? By America. President Wilson was the first great statesman who ever came to a world conference without one spark of racial prejudice. Infinitely much might have been hoped from that. But alas! he was 'all too human'; his noble ideals were vitiated by a parochial perspective, lack of experience in world politics, and a certain professorial vanity, which tried to do single-handed a work demanding all the strong hands and big hearts in America. The united brain of the United States! That must have solved the problem. That cold, clear brain, unvitiated by racial hatreds and distrust, had lifted the whole complex into the upper air. But it was never permitted to try. Wilson played a lone hand and it failed—as lone hands are apt to do. Since then America, seeing her failure, has righted it and, with a superb gesture and inspired by pure reason, has taken the Old World's hand again and set her feet on surer ground."

I perceived a growing dislike for Herr Strossmayer in the eyes of several among his listeners. A few were at no trouble to conceal it.

"And what does this veiled attack on our system amount to?" inquired Sir Bruce. "What, if it were not an impertinent question, do you seek in England for Jugo-Slavia, monsieur?"

He spoke suavely, but I knew that aversion from the stranger lay behind the question. The old Indian was deeply interested, however, and did not conceal the fact.

"The difficulty of a leader," answered Strossmayer, "is to find the brains of his nation and win them to himself, first by trust and then by enthusiasm. I am not a leader of men, but even in my quest, trust and enthusiasm are the vital need. I am in fact a tradesman, seeking to do a 'deal' in chemists. We regard young men of promise in the laboratory as potential gold mines, and since your chemistry in this country, despite the handicaps under which research labors, is still the finest and subtlest in the world, I come first to you. England has led the van a thousand times, and if you let your discoveries—synthetic dyes, for example—slip through your fingers, that is not to condemn the discoveries—only the greedy idiots who sold one of the most precious possessions in the world for immediate gain. I want your young, brilliant chemists—your men of single soul and pure ambition—who pass their examinations and attain honors, only to find themselves unhonored forever afterwards. I come to seek these men, who have left the retort and spectroscope behind and know the significance of the electroscope and spinthariscope—the men who may turn romance into reality and find the philosopher's stone in this our time."

"You will seek far," said General Fordyce. "We are a practical people."

"You believe so," answered the newcomer. "But you are mistaken in that self-estimate. Your genius is handicapped by your muddled thinking at every turn. A less practical or imaginative people never existed. And yet your absurd lack of imagination has enabled you to do deeds that beggar the imagination! I do not belittle your greatness for a moment, General. As to the chemists, they are here. As a radio-chemist myself, though without genius, I know enough to understand, and I find material waiting for me. Yes, the men are here, and the adequate rewards and inducements are in Jugo-Slavia."

"You would buy our devotion for your State?" I asked.

"Exactly. I say, 'Come and throw in your luck with us, my young friends. You will be in clover, because we understand your importance and know the prizes are gigantic, though few. Come and do your best; and whether you can help us, or fail to do so, you will be respected, honored, rewarded and put beyond the reach of anxiety while your unproductive work proceeds. We trust you, as ministers of Science, to pay faithful service in her courts; and if it is granted to you to do great things for Jugo-Slavia—well; but if you fail, then your failure and disappointment will be all you have to suffer. Your future in any case is assured. You are servants of the new State, responsible to none but your peers. You will receive handsome emolument and generous consideration, on the sole understanding that your brains are dedicated to your adopted country.'"

"You would tempt away our youthful geniuses?" asked Medland.

"Why put it so? If you do not want them, we do. Be sure that none will come to us from England, or anywhere else, if his native land offers him, or her, sufficient inducement to remain."

"Have you made a start, Mr. Strossmayer?" inquired Leon Jacobs.

"An excellent start," he answered. "I have found three first-rate men, three second-rate men, but of a useful stamp, and one superman—a young fellow worth ten thousand a year to any nation on earth."

"You are frank," declared Jack Smith.

"I can afford to be," answered the Jugo-Slav. "These men know the best they may hope from their own country; they are aware of the prizes that you offer; they know that if they enjoy phenomenal success and get appointed to great institutions, or even Departments of State, their future work will not be to their liking. Salaries and pensions carry small weight where there is a touch of genius. The big men want to do their own work; but once harnessed and shackled by the Government, their own work is the last thing they will ever have any more time or opportunity to do. When a great man reaches such resounding renown that your official world hears his name, he is appointed where he belongs, and henceforth his precious time, which ought to be worth thousands an hour, and might be worth millions, is devoted—to what? To the work by which he attained fame? To the slow, patient research which is helping the sum of human knowledge and potential prosperity? Far from it. He has become a Government official, and henceforth routine and red tape eat him alive. He does the mean tasks of a shopkeeper, runs his department as cheaply as possible, is heckled over wages, fettered with accounts—the price of raw material, the problems of labor, the wages of charwomen, the cost of coke. Every stupid thing he has to do but the thing he alone can do and ought alone to be doing. That's England's way with her men of science; and so we find more brain power of the highest order wasted here than in any other civilized country on earth."

Sir Bruce—an old civil servant—was able to confirm this indictment.

"I should like to contradict you if I could," he said bluntly. "But you are not far wrong. A Government demands results, sublimely indifferent to the causes which produce effects. Scientific research is ignored very grossly here, as elsewhere. Far deeper problems, of a moral nature, arise out of the situation than you guess, however."

"Very likely," answered Strossmayer. "But the first thing is to be practical and build up a basis of wealth and prosperity for our naked, newborn Jugo-Slavia. We proceed accordingly and feel no fear for our morals. It should be easy for a prosperous and educated people to be moral; not so easy for a hungry and illiterate nation."

He rattled on with sublime confidence in his ideals and then, looking at his watch, rose, made a very charming and comprehensive bow, and left us.

The impressions he created were, upon the whole, unfavorable, and I think only Jacobs and myself were in any sort attracted by the man. We recognized an agile mind, abundant enthusiasm, and a personality unfamiliar and beyond our experience. But with that none quarreled. It was the stranger's ironical attitude toward our country that annoyed most of us.

"To suggest that his semi-barbaric nation is wiser than we are, and proposes to take a saner course, can only be called offensive nonsense," declared General Fordyce.

"These astute foreigners have all got a bad streak," added Merrivale Medland. "I meet them in Spain and Portugal every year, and I know their little ways. I don't say he's a wrong 'un; but I'm not frightened, and I'm certainly not going to be down-hearted because Jugo-Slavia, or any other little rubbish heap, offers well-paid work to our young men who specialize in 'Stinks.'"

General Fordyce applauded these British sentiments; his brother did not.

"We found the chemists to win the war, and shall we not find the chemists to win the peace?" asked Jack Smith.

"A very pertinent question," answered Sir Bruce, "for when the radioactivity that lies in hiding comes actually within our reach and we discover also the power to apply it, then the world will be faced with one alternative alone to universal peace; and that is universal destruction. It follows that to let our young men of promise identify themselves with stranger nations is to reduce our hopes in the supreme direction."

"We must assume that England will discover the secret," declared General Fordyce, "for we are the only nation who can be trusted not to make a mess of it when we have. In fact such a power is unthinkable in any other hands than ours, and be sure Providence knows this as well as we do."

Chapter III

What Has Done It?

It was the third evening after the introduction of Paul Strossmayer to our little circle that poor Alexander Skeat had honored us with his company at dinner—and lectured us afterwards. For that is the only way to describe his minatory harangue. He treated us like a parcel of rather unsatisfactory children and, for my part, I doubted not that to his luminous and far-reaching mind the bulk of his fellow men appeared little removed from the immaturity of youth. Indeed we should have all conceded the point, if he had not been at such rather ill-bred pains to rub it in.

As Bishop Blore said, "Most men know well enough that they are mediocre; but they resent being told so by superior and scornful strangers."

I recollect that Mr. Skeat was troubled about the art of the country, and he cursed it in good set terms. Art was a subject whereon we were very willing to learn, and though General Fordyce, his brother, and others paid no great attention, a dozen members—Jacobs and myself included—listened with interest and found the famous publicist convincing and suggestive. It was left for our latest comer, Mr. Strossmayer, to turn the monologue into a discussion when he asked civilly but pointedly, why Art, in the mind of the visitor, shut out all greater present demands and immediate needs.

Skeat had just flouted Nature with hearty contempt.

"If she can be personified in human terms, then only a lunatic would applaud her hideous manifestations," he said, "since she destroys with one hand what she creates with the other. To Art we must look for any rational interpretation of Nature, or human nature either."

"But where are Art's rational interpretations?" asked Strossmayer. "Surely art is dead, or shall we say in a state of suspended animation? The hard times have killed it. Only minor poets twitter; the painters have rushed pell-mell into a blind alley, whence there is no escape save by the way back to Nature and her forms, which on the whole are more beautiful than any they attempt to make; music is in the hands of faddists and becomes as bodiless as dead wine; only the imitators of Chekov and Ibsen exist as serious dramatists; while the novelists are all bogged in psychoanalysis, which is a pathological rather than an artistic advance. So why not give weary Art a rest until wide-awake Science has had her say? Then, when Art is convalescent again, with a normal temperature and clear vision, she may find the world a place ripe for a new renaissance worthy of decent men and decent art."

"Idiot!" cried Alexander Skeat furiously. "Do you not understand that only through cleansing torrents and cathartic hurricanes of art the world can ever again become a place for anybody—decent or otherwise—to live in?"

He thundered on for full ten minutes, while his heavy eyebrows and bristling moustache vibrated with his emotion and his great jaw, like a bulldog's, seemed to grow squarer and squarer. He deluged us and the Jugo-Slav in a storm of hurtling and ferocious words; and finally challenged Strossmayer to elaborate his opinions.

His anger was doubtless in part theatrical, but when the foreigner described his own views and purposes, theories of applied science and ambitions to forward that application, Skeat became still more incensed.

"I shall oppose you heart and soul!" he promised. "I shall make public your pretensions and warn our young men to resist your malignant appeals. We are not yet a people to be suborned with Balkan gold."

"As a guest member of this club I speak to you; and you, too, are a guest member for this evening, therefore I have a right to demand confidence," replied Strossmayer quietly.

"I never listen to anybody in confidence," answered Skeat. "I am no longer a man. I am a European institution, and it is my function to survey the world from the watchtower of my own abnormal intelligence and proclaim my discoveries and opinions in all ears. These are perilous times for civilization, as I point out daily, and no man who approaches me must imagine the least respect for his intentions, or privacy for his plans. On your own showing you would rob the United Kingdom of an asset—an asset which I take leave to observe you grossly overvalue—for not by the road of Science and Reason shall man rise to the light, since Art and the Divine Afflatus are to be masters of the world. But nevertheless you do active wrong to tempt our youth, just as you err to suppose that the brute forces concealed in Nature will ever conquer man. It is a debased ideal and I shall fulminate against you."

Paul Strossmayer did not answer. He was annoyed and a flame lit his dark eyes for a moment; but he kept himself in hand and permitted Skeat to discuss another subject. Somebody—I think the bishop—discussed wealth, and Skeat took him up.

"I despair of showing people how to use wealth," he said. "They think because I choose to be poor, that I cannot possibly be an authority."

"Nobody knows how to use wealth," asserted General Fordyce, and for once the visitor found himself in agreement.

"Probably you are right, and the most well meaning are among our deepest failures," he answered. "Your Rockefellers and Carnegies do their best, as I honestly think; but their best is vitiated by domestic predilections and superstitions. Such men cannot remotely vision what belongs to the best. The problem is how, with increasing raw material—namely wealth—to turn it into that immaterial and precious finished product we understand by happiness."

"But if wealth cannot produce individual happiness, as every millionaire knows, how are we to turn it into universal happiness?" asked Leon Jacobs.

"By transforming it into human sympathy and understanding," answered Skeat. "Wealth admittedly puts the mind above a certain sort of primitive want. It wins security for the candlestick of the body, and enables us to turn our attention to the light of the soul, which should burn before all men from that candlestick. Having secured for the mass of humanity physical conditions long familiar to every pet dog, we proceed—"

"To what?" asked Strossmayer, who had bided his time.

"To Art."

The Jugo-Slav shook his head.

"Not so," he answered. "Not so, Mr. Alexander Skeat. To Science we must turn for the true application of wealth, just as we must look to Science for the creation of it."

"Pure Science is a selfless activity—the highest and noblest upon which a man's mind can concentrate," declared Jacobs.

Strossmayer applauded him and continued.

"What we in Jugo-Slavia want is a development of social science, inspired by the new possibilities, and a scientific application of the new wealth now being wickedly and fruitlessly squandered around us. The power of wealth is still terrific, and far the greater part is running to waste, even as the heat of the sun, or the forces of the tides."

"The wisdom of school children," retorted Skeat, "and to attempt to make you comprehend is vain, since you have not yet reached the starting point of reality, that only spirit quickeneth."

He rose then, declared that he must catch his train, enveloped himself in a great cloak and challenging hat, and prepared to depart.

"Read me," he said to Jacobs and myself as he bade us farewell. "Read me humbly; read what I have written; read with the determination to understand. Much you will not; much you may."

A week later, some of us were dining with General Fordyce at his private house, and the death of Skeat occupied our thoughts to the exclusion of all other subjects. Indeed there were probably not a dozen intelligent men met together in England, or the Continent, who did not find the mystery absorb their minds. Two prime considerations challenged mankind: first the manner of this departure and secondly the significance of Alexander Skeat himself as a force in the affairs of humanity.

Upon the second problem I recollect that Leon Jacobs spoke while the general's dinner party was in progress. There were present our host and his brother, Merrivale Medland, Bishop Blore, Jacobs and myself.

"I don't think it matters a button to the world whether he was in it or not," said Leon. "I speak impartially and recognize his genius. But, as a man, we have seen with our own eyes that he was absurdly vain, ill mannered, and discourteous. As an intellectual force he was a bully, and for his success relied on satire—a poor vehicle for preaching at best."

"Even so judged," declared the bishop, "Pope or Voltaire, Swift or Anatole France excel him both in art and poignancy."

"He destroyed, but created nothing," continued Jacobs. "And, after all, what do his lectures and books amount to? What is the sum total of his message? Only that most people are born fools; which we knew already."

I contested this sweeping criticism and endeavored to show how Skeat had influenced modern thought; but none supported me and General Fordyce pointed out that the dead man had always stood outside life and been contented to laugh at the show from a comfortable seat in the auditorium.

"His real value and significance cannot be judged by his own generation," declared Medland, "and whether he will interest the next is exceedingly doubtful. Most likely the principal attraction that he will offer is the manner of his death; and I, for one, by no means discredit the policeman's description of a strange beast. There's no smoke without fire, and the creature known as a vampire didn't win its universal fame through superstition alone. Be sure there's something in it. A skeptical generation wants shaking up, and to be reminded that there are more things, even on earth still, than are dreamed of in our philosophy."

We chaffed the wine merchant, who was addicted to spiritualism and of a credulous mind in everything except his own business; but General Fordyce reminded us how Medland stood not alone in his belief—that some unknown animal might, after all, be responsible for the extraordinary wound by which Skeat had perished. Policeman Syme's description of a huge bird, or bat, seen dimly through the midnight murk of the park obtained a certain measure of credence; for the vulpine smell, reported by four other independent witnesses beside himself, suggested a possibility of some monstrous, flying reptile, or mammal, failing any more plausible explanation.

We challenged Sir Bruce, as an authority second to none, upon the subject, and, to my surprise, he did not express himself with any certainty. He was guarded, but preserved an open mind.

"You know more about bats and such creatures than any living man, Sir Bruce," said Bishop Blore. "Can you conceive of the possibility of some survival from geological days reappearing in the twentieth century?"

"So stated, the phenomena sound more mad than ever," declared Jacobs; but the man of science showed no impatience before the fantastic problem.

"Common sense naturally inclines one to laugh the proposition out of court," he said; "but reason is always guarded, and because a thing on the face of it looks grotesque, impossible, or absurd, Science will not be contented to leave it at that. Much appears grotesque and absurd from a human point of view, which in itself is perfectly rational, logical and seemly. The deepsea creatures have faces that are hideous, or absurd, in the eyes of unthinking man, or child. I remember myself, in tender youth, finding a crab in a pool, whose countenance haunted me and produced nightmares for six weeks. Yet it was without doubt a face perfectly adapted to the requirements of the bearer. The face of an octopus appears to us beyond measure sinister and forbidding. We loathe its parrot beak and cold, inhuman eye; but only because it is in another category of creation than our own and its manner of life and method of taking food repulse us. A spider is no more horrible.

"I am not prepared entirely to discard the possible existence of living beings outside our own experience and as yet unreported in nature. There have always been giants in the world of unconscious life, as there have been among human beings; and we know that only recently rumors have reached Science, from out-of-the way regions in central Africa and South America, of gigantic living creatures—possible survivals of prehistoric forms. There may be life in the uttermost depths of the sea, in the equatorial jungles, and in remote polar regions, as yet undiscovered by man. It is not contrary to reason to suspect that much; nor is it wholly beyond possibility that some individual of an unknown species might break from its environment and appear for the first time to conscious eyes. Such achievement would of course be easier for a winged mammal, or reptile, than any other creature."

Medland was delighted. "If we believers in a dragon have you on our side—" he began, but Sir Bruce stopped him.

"You must not say that I am on your side. Every reasonable supposition points to a contrary conclusion from yours; and in any case we may very safely suspend judgment; for, supposing that this is not a phantom of the policeman's imagination, but a living thing, what follows?"

"It follows that the beggar was hungry, perhaps, and didn't kill poor Skeat for wickedness, but supper," suggested General Fordyce.

"Exactly, Hugh," replied his brother. "Assuming that we deal with an animal, then we must suppose the brute was hunting for food. It strikes down its prey—sublimely unaware of the distinguished fellow creature it has destroyed—and is about to make its meal when interrupted."

"Just what I think," declared Medland. "That's my theory. The thing kills Skeat in some peculiar way, by a sort of stab with a beak or claw, and then is going to devour him, or far more likely suck his blood. For everything points to a vampire. But I go farther and ask who is to say that the creature is not controlled by a discarnate human will that inhabits it?"

We laughed loudly; while Medland, who was read in all manner of medieval nonsense on this subject, poured chapter and verse into our ears.

"One would think that you had been on intimate terms with vampires," I said.

Then Leon Jacobs asked a question. "To come back from fairy tales to facts—what, if anything, is known about blood-sucking animals, Sir Bruce! One has heard, of course, of vampire bats, but do such things exist in reality? And if so, have they been known to touch a human being? Medland vows his mass of evidence must stand for more than myth; but you cannot winnow grain out of chaff alone—however large the quantity of chaff. What is the truth on the subject?"

"Bats there certainly are that suck blood," admitted Sir Bruce, "and other bats, of more ferocious appearance and greater size, that have an evil reputation which they never earned. *Vampyrus spectrum*, the false vampire, and others belonging to the genus *phyllostoma* are perfectly harmless 'leaf-nosed' bats from South America. The true vampires are also South American. Their incisors and canine teeth are modified for flesh cutting; their stomachs are small and their intestines short and not adapted for any other food than blood. There is, however, no mystery about the way these vamparines feed, and I must record one unfortunate fact: the most famous and authentic bloodsucker of man, *Desmodus rufus*, a red-brown, tailless bat, is only three inches long—one of the smallest species. Its bite carries no venom and is less dangerous than that of a rat."

"We certainly cannot imagine a specimen of *Desmodus rufus* swelled to the size of a bullock," said Bishop Blore. Then he continued. "One thing is pretty obvious. If the creature exists, food he must certainly eat, and if his provender depends upon other animals, we shall hear of him again before long. In the event of such a monster appearing among us, it will demand not merely a pint of blood occasionally, but pretty deep draughts. It follows that we shall meet the wretch again tolerably soon; and if we do not, then we may agree with the majority—that no such abominable thing has in reality been seen."

"And the manner of Skeat's death would then be illuminated," declared Merrivale Medland. "I mean if other victims occur; for then we shall probably learn what is the cause and nature of this strange wound and end by catching the bat itself. Already the creature may have killed sheep, or cattle in lonely places and drunk its fill."

We laughed again at the wine merchant's idea, and ere long the party broke up. Medland and the bishop went one way, while Jacobs and I saw Sir Bruce to his bungalow, which stood on the hillside in its own small grounds. It was a building of one story with a flat roof, partly glazed, and in summertime we often spent an evening on the top of it under awnings; for an observatory with a good equatorial telescope occupied one end, Sir Bruce being an amateur astronomer among his other activities.

He spoke as we went along of Medland's credulity and sighed for human nature, that so willingly preserved its legends and follies sprung from the childhood of mankind.

"Education cannot kill what most of us learn at our mother's knees," he said. "That is the receptive period, and just in the vital years, when reason should be honored, we load the infant mind with supernatural nonsense, which unhappily sticks in ninety-nine cases out of a hundred. A really reasonable man might appear to most of us almost as inhuman as the octopus of which we spoke; for his attitude to life would infallibly be guided by ideals and arguments still foreign to our best hopes. Reason is stifled and choked off at every turn."

"You can trust no man to be reasonable," admitted Jacobs, "though, no doubt, each of us imagines himself to be the most reasonable person on earth."

"In nothing does our unreason more appear than in our private opinion of ourselves," confessed Sir Bruce. Then we left him at his door and went homeward to the bachelor diggings we shared.

No light was thrown upon the death of Alexander Skeat, and nothing further heard of the chimera assumed to have destroyed him. Chemical analysis showed a prodigious alteration in the constituents of the dead man's blood and revealed a mineral substance, akin to one of the radioactive elements, developed in it; but the reason for such an extraordinary change was hidden, and what had entered by the thread-like orifice to destroy life, science could not detect.

Rumors came that the apparition of a flying monster had been seen both in Surrey and in Yorkshire; yet investigation ended in nothing trustworthy. Meantime London felt no alarm, while maintaining an active interest for longer than it condescends, as a rule, to devote to any solitary sensation. Everybody supposed that

Skeat would have left a direction to be cremated; therefore, since he never conformed to public opinion and delighted to refute general conclusions, he had done no such thing. His relations buried him at Kensal Green, and the greatest living sculptor declined to design the tomb, because Skeat had insulted him during the previous year.

Londoners were said to walk less in the parks after dark; but if that were true of certain nervous individuals, it certainly did not apply to the mass, who make the green spaces of the metropolis their thoroughfares.

The actual spot where Skeat had fallen and the neighboring region from which the flying monster was declared to have ascended were subject to intelligent scrutiny; but not a clue of any sort rewarded it. John Syme had vowed the creature hopped twice, and if his narrative were true, it appeared probable that some mark of the operation must surely appear; but no trace of any impress was recorded on the winter herbage, and the detectives, together with the public at large, soon regarded the alleged apparition as a feat of imagination on the constable's part. It was left to a later date to restore credence in Policeman Syme and reawaken the curiosity and alarm of the metropolis.

Chapter IV

The Albert Memorial

Nothing is more puzzling to me than the attitude of a man to his friend's friend. I have often wondered why people for whom I entertained the greatest regard, and who reciprocated my attachment as heartily, should yet number among their closest companions and confidants somebody else whom I detested. And my friends have observed the same phenomenon in connection with myself. Doubtless we are all built up in different facets and echo different flashes from our fellow creatures. Thus, when Leon Jacobs began to develop an active understanding and comradeship with the Jugo-Slav, Paul Strossmayer, I was not indeed perturbed or jealous—but the fact caused me to wonder. The comradeship did not extend to much beyond conversation at the club, for both men were exceedingly busy and their operations lay in different directions; but a certain quality of mind was common to both: they found themselves reflecting life from the same angle and each, I think, was eminently endowed with that faculty of reason, the lack of which in human affairs, Sir Bruce Fordyce so often and so feelingly deplored.

Nor did I myself find Strossmayer antipathetic, for the judgment of Leon Jacobs was good enough for me; but I never understood the stranger as well, or shared his ideals so fully as did Leon. My insular bent of mind preserved an element of doubt and suspense concerning him until we became far better acquainted, and though I never shared the dislike and suspicion openly expressed at the Club of Friends behind Strossmayer's back in the light of subsequent events, I was not at first prepared to champion Strossmayer through thick and thin, as Jacobs did.

The man certainly challenged us, and it was hard to feel indifferent towards him. Indeed the majority disliked him for his self-assertion—a trait always offensive to the average Englishman—and as time passed I was constrained to mark that, despite his plea for reason, Sir Bruce shared to the full his brother's concealed aversion towards the new member.

I think, perhaps unconsciously, the warning of dead Alexander Skeat influenced some of us. He had hated Strossmayer, and there is no doubt that Jack Smith and possibly others grew in time to associate the foreigner with Skeat's death.

As a matter of fact, so far as his comments and opinions on the subject went, Paul Strossmayer appeared absolutely indifferent to the end of the great publicist. He merely reiterated a former opinion, that Skeat was better dead than alive, and he took no part in my hearing upon the interminable discussions of the mystery that followed; but then happened another sensation that banished the death of Skeat from men's minds, and London gasped before such a wonder as it had never experienced until now. This new shock did wake up Strossmayer to some purpose and he declared a theory with which Science speedily found itself in complete agreement. Indeed, before phenomena so unique and beyond all previous human experience, it appeared that only one theory was admissible.

On a night near the end of the year, there fell down that great memorial in Hyde Park erected to the Consort of her late Majesty, Queen Victoria. Yet to say that the Albert Memorial fell down is hardly a correct statement. The huge affair, with its central statue, canopy and elaborate decorative groups of sculptured, emblematic figures, was destroyed so strangely that it would be more correct to say it was pulverized, than that it fell down.

At half past two, on a clear December night, the police in the neighborhood heard a long-drawn, hissing and rendering sound, but nothing to be described as an explosion. It was, they declared, as though a torrent of water descended—the liquid rush of a waterfall. Terrific forces were applied to the memorial, and they left the mass of it redistributed. The monument ceased to exist; but in its place was no such chaos of shattered pillars, broken masonry and dismembered statues as an explosion must have wrought. Such a spectacle as the war had rendered only too familiar was not here. No haphazard ruin appeared before the dazed sight of the night watchers who collected round it. Instead they were faced with a huge, conical pile of fine dust. It was as though the Albert Memorial had been lifted bodily from its roots in the earth, set in some gigantic mortar and brayed to powder, then poured out again upon the original site.

All London visited the gray pile next morning and a thousand explanations of this extraordinary metamorphosis occupied men's minds. The energy responsible for the change had worked within limits clearly defined. It had operated as smoothly as the cut of a knife. There was no surrounding disturbance. A few adjacent trees were burned as to their nearest boughs by the great heat produced by this instantaneous disintegration, but no evidences of explosive matter marked the scene. Only a little mountain of fine dust towered in place of the familiar monument, and a preliminary scientific assumption received universal acceptation. It was quite clear that energies beyond all experience had produced these results. They resembled in no way those created by the highest explosives as yet discovered and applied; nor did their operation place them in the same category with any known power. They worked differently and liberated an infinitely greater volume of force. Whether the stroke had come from earth or air none could assert; but Science held that air had freed the energy and rained it directly down upon the doomed memorial.

Examination of the elemental dust of stone and metal to which all had been reduced, revealed a startling chemical fact. The material had suffered radical changes. The force directed against it was responsible, not only for turning all into the smallest constituent particles; but had actually modified the matter, imparting novel attributes that neither stone nor metal before possessed.

It was left for the genius of a foreigner to link this extraordinary circumstance with another, and I shall return to the point in a moment.

First, however, one must record the impression conveyed and the emotion awakened in London by the event. "Catastrophe" it can hardly be called, for no actual public regret was expressed by any journal or man of authority. Indeed artists openly rejoiced in the disappearance of the memorial, and a tentative proposal to rebuild it on the old model received no support from any responsible person. But the smaller question of the thing itself was entirely lost in the larger one of the reason for its disappearance; for all men felt that what mattered was not the vanished object, but the unknown powers that had caused it to vanish.

The discussion centered upon one point. Was the world faced with a deliberate manifestation of consciously directed action; or did it behold the accidental effect of some physical phenomenon? Had some wandering vehicle of huge radioactivity penetrated our atmosphere and struck by chance, or was the incident the work of intelligent beings? The general opinion, the wish being father to the hope, no doubt, inclined to a belief that an aerolite of great size had reached earth and liberated thereon properties of matter as yet only in the dawn of their human discovery; but a more highly educated conclusion opposed this belief and very definitely declared the destruction of the monument to be a work of conscious beings. Some of these inquirers (inspired by ingenious works of fiction) went so far as to affirm possible interference from extra-terrestrial causes; but the more reasonable thinkers suspected that human agency must be responsible—an opinion hardly less disturbing than the other. The humorous aspect of the event was not ignored, and I recollect that, within our own circle, Jacobs pointed out the discrepancy between the prodigious powers marshaled to destroy the Albert Memorial and the insignificant object itself.

"It is as though somebody had taken a fifteen-inch gun to shoot a rabbit," he said; and it was upon the same occasion, at the club, that an increasing interest and divergence of opinions upon the subject of Paul Strossmayer were advanced in the one case and widened in the other, by himself. We had not seen him since the incident in Hyde Park; but perceived, when he did reappear among us, that he had taken it far more to heart than any Englishman. He was tremendously impressed by what had happened; and he was also depressed, for he told us frankly that, in his opinion, certain unknown persons had stolen a march upon him, his friends and their hopes.

"I need not trouble you with my own fears," he said, in answer to a question, "but I may say that my 'super-chemist,' as I call him, shares my view. Ian Noble believes that a tremendous secret advance has been made along the line of radioactive research, and he suspects that this apparently senseless operation is no more than a private experiment with a newly discovered energy."

"Then why such a senseless and mischievous outrage?" asked General Hugh Fordyce. "I know nothing of art, but the Albert Memorial stood for something far more important than art. It commemorated a famous and dignified personage—a royal character of whom nothing but good can be spoken. Moreover he was the grandfather of the reigning monarch, and there is, therefore, an element of disloyalty in such a performance that must make any decent man prefer to believe that it happened by chance and was an accident. If otherwise, then an enemy to England is responsible."

"Be sure those that did this thing were not concerned with the memory of the late Prince Albert," replied Strossmayer. "Very probably they never heard of him. We cannot tell whence they come, or what their purposes are. Ian Noble inclines to believe that they are in our midst; and he takes a grave view of the event, for it is clear that these people are concealing their discovery from the rest of civilization. In any case he suspects that we shall not be left long in doubt."

We argued the point and Bishop Blore was very positive that no conscious agency would be found responsible.

"In a sense," he said, "we may regard the mystery as on all fours with that which preceded it and is already nearly forgotten. I mean the death of Alexander Skeat. As Sir Bruce pointed out in that connection, had some actual, living, but unconscious, thing destroyed the man, it could only have done so for its own needs and to satisfy the physical craving of hunger. In that case it must have been heard of again quickly. But it has not been heard of again, and we justly assume, therefore, that 'the Bat,' as the newspapers called it, was a myth. The same position is created here. If this is the work of men who have become possessed of new knowledge, then they will not stop at this childish performance. It is now some days since the monument in Hyde Park was destroyed, but we have not heard of any similar disaster. Therefore I cherish a growing conviction that this event is natural and offers us a glimpse into some operations of nature denied the world until the present time. Tremendous energy has descended from space, and chance directed it upon England, upon London, upon Hyde Park, upon the Albert Memorial. It entered our atmosphere—this foreign body—from limitless space and braved the perils of combustion, or may have largely suffered from them. Yet no great fireball, or shooting star, or other celestial visitor was reported. We may assume, then, that this aggregation of unknown matter this unfamiliar element launched upon us found the atmosphere harmless to affect it. The mass—it may have been great; it may have been small—strikes an object composed of terrestrial material—marble and metal—and instantly it transforms all to dust."

"And more than that," added Jack Smith, "it transmutes these familiar things and imparts to them a quality which was not there before."

Some agreed with the bishop, and I confess my inclination made me do so, since only along a line of natural interpretation lay peace of mind for humanity. We were left in suspense and Strossmayer declared again that such suspense would be of short duration. Bishop Blore's theory reduced him to silence for a while; but, as he confessed afterwards, it did in reality something very significant and flashed a light into his mind, which took the shape of a letter to *The Times*.

At the moment, however, he gave no sign of his inspiration. We asked him concerning his "super-chemist" and he was apparently quite frank upon that subject. Indeed the Jugo-Slav's candor always inclined Jacobs and myself towards him. We believed in it from the first—especially Leon Jacobs; but Medland, General Fordyce, Sir Bruce and Bishop Blore declared that Strossmayer's ingenuous attitude was assumed deliberately and by no means represented the real man. They held it a mask—a stalking-horse of unreality—behind which he pursued his own purposes. For they reminded us that the stranger did not always choose to be artless and had a convenient way of failing sometimes to hear a pertinent question. Their suspicions, indeed, gained ground and point during subsequent events and Strossmayer's letter to *The Times,* which appeared two days later, while it strengthened my conviction that he was honest, served to establish opposite conclusions in the minds of most of us.

For the moment Paul Strossmayer spoke of Ian Noble in response to our questions. He praised the young man's genius and declared that he was already on the track of great discoveries. He also temporarily disarmed doubt by promising to bring Noble to the club upon a future evening.

"If you are not tired of great men—for a great man he is—I shall invite him to dinner presently," he promised. "And then you will meet a rare personality, one, as I believe, destined to future honors and distinction—in Jugo-Slavia."

We promised his protégé a hearty welcome, and after Strossmayer's departure again debated the foreigner's puzzling personality.

Merrivale Medland committed himself to a strong suspicion and, to my surprise, Sir Bruce and the bishop supported him. "The man's a humbug and thinks he's fooling us," declared our wine merchant with conviction. "What's more, I believe he knows a great deal about this business—perhaps all about it."

"Time will probably show," admitted Sir Bruce. "I do not like the man for this reason: he is a gross materialist. His ambitions are mean and he is concerned only for Jugo-Slavia and himself. Despite certain feeble protestations to the contrary, he is not moved by any enthusiasm for humanity at large; and did he and his scientific slaves really hit upon those latent radioactive energies presently destined to transform the face of the world and make, or mar, civilization, I do not for a moment believe that he and his immature and backward people could be trusted to employ it for the welfare of all. They would use it to erect a barrier of personal advantage between themselves and mankind. They would seek to put themselves on a pedestal, threaten all other nations and exploit their discovery to the disadvantage of their neighbors and the world at large."

"One cannot forget that Alexander Skeat, who, whatever else he may have been, was a profound student of human nature, warned us very forcibly against Strossmayer. We have Granger's word for it," said Bishop Blore.

"He certainly said so," I replied. "Both Jacobs and I heard him. We set it down to a personal animosity, because Paul Strossmayer did not fear to contradict him."

"But you have to remember also," Jacobs reminded them, "that Strossmayer has often spoken of all men in a friendly and kindly spirit. He is a patriot, I grant; but one can admit no direct word fairly creating a suspicion that Strossmayer would 'exploit' a discovery, as Sir Bruce says, to the disadvantage of other nations, even though he might naturally desire his own people should gain first and principal advantage."

"For that matter, Sir Bruce," I asked, "supposing that the energy were really ready and waiting for the world, into whose hands would you place it with absolute conviction that you were doing well and wisely?"

"A tremendous question," answered Jacobs.

"No question at all," replied General Hugh. "My dear fellow, can there be a shadow of doubt as to the reply? Emphatically England, and England alone, could be trusted with, such a terrific responsibility. If you want an analogy, look at the Seven Seas. To whom could the dominion of the ocean be entrusted but ourselves? None but a fool entertains two opinions."

We laughed at our archaic friend and reminded him of the Washington Conference; but he held it no laughing matter; and then, two days later, our interest was aroused by the Jugo-Slav's letter to *The Times*. It did a thing as yet not done, and directly linked the death of Alexander Skeat with the destruction of the Albert Memorial.

I transcribe this important communication, for those best able to judge considered it a valuable statement, calculated to throw considerable light on the problem, now conflicting with other and more vital social difficulties that disturbed England.

To the Editor, *The Times*

"Sir: One aspect of the singular occurrence in Hyde Park should be the subject of special examination. And as such a line of inquiry may prove fruitful, I venture to propose it.

"Briefly I am of opinion that some connection exists between the death of Mr. Alexander Skeat and the destruction of the memorial to the late Prince Consort; and my reason for this suspicion will be found on examination of the details in each case. For what do we learn? The monument and the man were alike obliterated by some unfamiliar means, and while the remains of the work of art bear testimony not only to destruction but transmutation of constituents, so, in the case of the man, a profound and inexplicable alternation is recorded in the physical material of which his body was composed. The bone and the blood alike afforded examples of an extraordinary alteration.

"We find, then, that to the familiar substances of stone and iron, flesh and blood, there has been applied a force, or energy, to which in human knowledge they have never before been exposed, since it produces upon them unfamiliar, but parallel, phenomena; and we may therefore assume, not unreasonably, that both the monument and the man were subjected to different charges of a similar application.

"'We have obtained evidence,' says Professor Soddy, our greatest living authority on radioactive elements, 'that in the atoms of matter exists a store of energy beyond comparison greater than any over which we have obtained control. In the slow changes of the radioactive elements there is known to be an evolution of energy nearly a million times as great as has ever been obtained from a similar weight of matter before.'

"Now, sir, I submit that something very like this has happened, and I venture to believe that a close connection can be established between the two events above mentioned. Granted that both acts were the work of conscious intellect, and deliberate, not accidental, then a considerable step may be made along the correct line of investigation; though since no conceivable connection of motive can be established between the murder of Skeat (if murder it be) and the downfall of the monument, we may have to wait for further manifestations before it is possible to prove deliberate purpose.

“In connection with the unknown properties of the radioactive elements still to be discovered, I may conclude with a brief reference to one famous product already known and employed. Spectrum analysis revealed its existence before any of its properties were appreciated and still much concerning them is doubtful; but one thing appears established. In all radioactive changes two ultimate products appear: helium and lead. Chemists have established the existence of lead in the blood of Mr. Skeat and in the dust of the monument.

Of radium, the best-known radioactive element, the story is fairly familiar; but few of the intelligent public yet appear to be aware that helium, which can be easily produced in vast quantities, has already been harnessed to the service of man. Having discovered the existence of this element in the sun, Science began to hunt for it on earth, and was speedily rewarded. Palmieri found traces in the lava of Vesuvius; Hillebrand, in the United States, extracted small quantities from a rare mineral, and in 1895, Sir William Ramsay also found it. Yet, until 1918, but a few cubic yards of helium had been collected. This was, however, enough to determine its qualities and prove that, after hydrogen, helium furnished the lightest gas known to Science, and—a greater asset—that it was nonflammable and nonexplosive. These facts may possibly throw light on the event in Hyde Park. Subsequently vast stores of helium gas were discovered amid the mineral products of Alberta and New Brunswick, and means invented for their extraction and purification. Ten million cubic feet of helium can now be annually obtained from Alberta alone—a quantity sufficient to keep at least two large airships in regular commission.

"Here, then, is one mighty available force familiar already to Science, and who shall declare that some other and still more tremendous energy has not already been discovered by the mind of man and revealed in the recent extraordinary occurrences? Unknown states of matter of course exist, and the conditions and properties of even familiar elements under those states—e.g., of extreme heat, or cold—offer rich ground of research as yet unexplored.

"Faithfully yours,

"Paul Strossmayer

"(Of the Jugo-Slavia Commission.)"

This letter excited a good deal of interest and elicited considerable correspondence, though it led to nothing practical in connection with the mysteries responsible for it. Various learned men agreed with Strossmayer; others differed from him; but in many minds he certainly succeeded in connecting the two disasters. Inquiry along that line, however, threw no light whatever on the agents of either, and not a shadow of clue rewarded the professional exertions of the police, or the amateur activities of many individuals. There remained only the voice of Science, to prove those curious atomic transmutations of the destroyed substances in man and stone already recorded.

As for the effect of Strossmayer's letter upon our little community at the Club of Friends, it did not serve to change opinion, but if anything, increased the suspicion generally entertained against him.

"He would not know so much, if he did not know a great deal more," declared General Fordyce. "Rest assured his letter is merely bluff—a blind to distract suspicion from himself."

"So I think," added Merrivale Medland. "There appears no method in his madness yet; but wait and see."

"While we are waiting he may overrun civilization," declared Bishop Blore. "It is a grave question in my mind, whether we should not impart our suspicions to the authorities and at least put the man under surveillance."

"What on earth could we say?" I asked; and Sir Bruce agreed with me, that no reasonable ground existed for such a step.

"I, too, distrust and dislike him," he confessed; "but for reasons profoundly different from your own, Bishop. I do not suspect that Strossmayer is responsible for these operations; but I do think he may be on the track of a vast unknown energy capable of overturning civilization, as you suggest. And did such awful power fall into his hands, I am convinced that he would put it to no altruistic or honorable purpose. That I believe; but I also believe that he and his friends have not yet reached the goal, and heartily I hope they may never do so."

Chapter V

Joseph Ashlar

Events which now rose on the forefront of national politics darkened the future and threatened to precipitate in storm the clouds long hanging heavily over our industrial progress and content. Their tragic promise banished every lesser consideration and it is not too much to say that the curious incidents already recorded had been entirely dismissed from thought by the mass of mankind, when a new sensation suddenly linked the social unrest of the hour with things already receding to forgetfulness in memory.

In the welter of the times and the slow and difficult readjustment of understanding and good will between Capital and Labor, dangers that had promised to dissolve suddenly increased ten thousand fold and society was plunged into ferment of doubt and fear by the threat of direct action from a key industry.

It was the mightiest, weightiest threat that Government had been called to face, and as a result of indifference to the well-known Bolshevist activities, that had spent a hundred thousand pounds upon propaganda in the country and deluged every industrial center with undesirable aliens, often introduced under a crafty system of false passports, the ruling authority found itself at last within measurable distance of revolution—a revolution, moreover, not destined to follow democratic lines, but such an upheaval as the usurper who reigned in Russia had openly indicated to his supporters of the United Kingdom. Other nations, more acutely alive to the awful peril, had set up barriers against it. Italy, France, America were safe, thanks to the exertions of longsighted and steadfast men; but England drifted steadily into the extremity of peril, and no hand was lifted to arrest or denounce one member of the industrious throng now working in secret for their master.

Labor had entered upon a phase of assertion and dictation, which could only end in one thing. Convinced that the nation, as a whole, was now alive to the hopeless futility of a Labor Government and conscious that pre-war ambitions in that direction might be dismissed from any practical scheme, Labor set forth to formulate demands that the other ranks of society could not concede save by an act of suicide.

Absolute Trade Unionism was on its way to become uncrowned king and destroy the fabric of the Constitution; indeed men among its leaders, until now contented to advance their ideals by recognized means of progress, abandoned their former attitude and openly declared that the "Constitution" itself was an elastic term capable of wider interpretation and other values than those accorded to it in the past.

The Prime Minister, the Hon. Erskine Owen, had undoubtedly encouraged this poisoning of the fountainheads by the process of private interviews followed by public concessions, and at this moment, aware perhaps of the abyss above which he stood, Owen suddenly took a firm stand with the opposing forces. It was high time, yet his definite and final attitude had occasioned acute surprise among the representatives of Labor; and Joseph Ashlar, their protagonist, who bulked large in the public eye, found himself in a quandary. He had already claimed a victory of stupendous significance; but he had spoken too soon and now stood in a difficult position supported by his own side, but without any national sympathy.

Joseph Ashlar was a demagogue of genius, sprung from the ranks of the Electrical Engineers. He had won immense concessions for his own trade and incidentally for others. He had already lessened the powers of Parliament and reached a point in his career when he believed the battle won. As in Russia the Duma had been destroyed by the Bolshevists and their Soviet system, so now in England the elected of the nation began to lose their authority under the ceaseless pressure of a resolute and remorseless trades unionism that leant steadily to the left.

Things were come to a crisis, and upon no question concerning his own union—upon no question directly involving Labor at all—Joseph Ashlar had thrown down the gauntlet. He stood proclaimed as a dictator for the whole of the workers, and he had chosen a subject for the challenge well calculated to rally many independent interests to his side. Upon the general question of British foreign administration, Ashlar demanded and, of course, secured an opportunity for debate. The Foreign Estimates offered an occasion, and armed with the authority of Labor's millions, Ashlar, who led his party in the House, declared the intention of calling a universal strike did the Government decline his demand to leave Mesopotamia and modify its control of India and Egypt.

It was a deliberate intention to establish minority rule, and England understood that no alternative could be submitted. Battle had been joined once and for all, and many thinkers rejoiced that suspense was at last at an end and the long threatened trial had to be faced and fought. Then, upon the night before the giant trial, Joseph Ashlar perished suddenly.

He resided at Battersea, and it was his custom at all seasons in the year to walk in the local park for half an hour, or longer, before retiring. A level path that ran near the ornamental waters was sacred to the great leader and had long been known in the district as "Ashlar's Walk." And here, where he had perambulated and revolved his projects for many years, death overtook him.

Just before nine o'clock on the evening before the vital debate, a policeman, upon his beat not far distant, heard a single loud cry and responded swiftly. He had already seen Joseph Ashlar proceeding to his accustomed exercise, saluted him, and given him "good night." What followed appeared a repetition in almost every respect of the events that attended the tragedy in St. James's Park. The officer found the victim lying face downward beside the ornamental waters. His arms were stretched out and his cap had fallen into the lake. He was either dead, or unconscious, and as the policeman knelt, to lift him and satisfy himself that it was indeed the famous demagogue, he became sensible of an extraordinary, animal smell heavy in the air around him—the reek of some living, carnivorous creature. The fox-like odor emanated from no particular quarter and, lowering Ashlar to the ground again, the constable turned his lantern about him. It was a clear, starry night with frost in the air, but as yet no resultant fog.

A clump of bamboos stood by the water's edge at a distance of thirty yards behind the fallen man, and turning his light in this direction, the constable was aware of some dark object behind the thicket. He hastened to obtain a nearer view, then became conscious of a pair of large, fiery eyes at the height of a tall man, as he described it, watching him through the canes. He hesitated, but conceiving it his duty to proceed, did so, vigorously blowing his whistle at the same time.

Now he distinctly saw a black mass "as large as a horse" squatting in the bamboos. Above it was lifted a sloping head on a long neck and, from this, shone the luminous eyes of a living thing. It was clearly alarmed and made no effort to attack the constable. Instead, as he asserted, it laid back its ears and appeared to shorten its neck, then leapt forward twice, crunching the canes and splashing the mire in which they grew. It now stood clear and, just as the sound of running feet came with welcome to the policeman's ear, the black monster opened a pair of wings and shot aloft. It zigzagged like a gigantic snipe, and disappeared into the sky, leaving an odor behind it that overpowered the air for an hour.

The constable declared that he heard no sound save the hiss of the air against the creature's body. It was like the exaggerated stroke of a carrier pigeon's wing. Otherwise, to use the watcher's own words again, "it was silent as an owl."

Turning to the fallen man, the police, for three were now upon the spot, lifted him and carried him to a seat. There seemed little doubt that he was dead, and they conveyed the inert, stalwart body between them to the constabulary station. But a doctor could only pronounce life extinct, while subsequent examination repeated in every particular the extraordinary phenomena reported on the death of Alexander Skeat. The dictator of the people had been stabbed in the breast by some pin-point weapon which had penetrated to the lungs. A thread-like wound could be traced from his right nipple inwards; while subsequent chemical analysis proved a repetition of the changed constituents of every bone in Ashlar's body and a profound disorganization of the flesh. Either some transmutation had taken place and matter pertaining to lead actually been created by the impact of the unknown energy, or else the energy itself had introduced a mineral into the dead man's tissue in a form outside all experience. That the latter theory was reasonable won denial from Science, and those best able to judge declared for transmutation. But such details occupied little general attention before the greater sensation of Joseph Ashlar's end and the reappearance of the nocturnal monster already reported and derided. Now the few who had believed in "the Bat" triumphed, and of our circle Merrivale Medland claimed attention and gave himself great airs for his faith.

"Only an obstinate idiot can hold out longer," he declared. "We have the word of the most skilful surgeons that the wound contains some sort of stuff deadly destructive to animal tissue, and that it is only of a thread-like nature, having length but no breadth. What known weapon could inflict such a wound? Even a hat pin would have created something more conspicuous. So it follows this vampire, as I believe it to be, has a natural weapon, perhaps a sting—perhaps a stabbing tongue—something with which it can instantly destroy its prey. But the poison so far evades analysis and, as we know, infusions of this infected blood produce death and similar symptoms in a milder form in inferior, hot-blooded animals. The cause of death in every case is immediate syncope; but the reason for such collapse cannot be explained any more than the operation of this unknown venom which causes it. Twice the creature has slain a victim, and twice been driven away the moment afterwards. Then who can longer doubt that it kills to live, and will soon make a further attempt with better luck?"

Yet many, of course, continued to doubt, for the destruction of Joseph Ashlar could not be considered a coincidence, or any unpremeditated action, whatever the agent responsible for it. Not only did this murder serve to dispel the idea of chance, which had guided argument on both sides in the problem of Alexander Skeat, but by doing so, lifted the whole mystery on to a higher and more terrible plane. For this stroke indicated many things directly calculated to oppose the theory of some unknown matter accidentally loosed upon civilization. It indicated deliberation and purpose. Joseph Ashlar had been slain for very sufficient reasons, and a conscious hand was responsible for his destruction. Men, not an animal, had killed him. "The Bat" merely confused the issue. The mystery from the first challenged England far less shrewdly than the fact itself. That Joseph Ashlar was dead, on the eve of his great battle, appeared a more tremendous event than any details of his end. A wave of feeling swept the United Kingdom and a very ugly temper developed in the North. For the proletariat argued that this stroke was official—a direct retort to their own threat of direct action, and an indication that two, if necessary, could play the same game. The immediate effect at least proved salutary, for the extremists were cowed by the loss of Joseph Ashlar; the result of his death proved a definite setback for the "Red" Labor Party and fear crept into their councils. Some return of peace marked the social situation and the threatened danger receded behind the horizon of politics for a season.

But Joseph Ashlar's death awoke far deeper emotions than either of the mysteries that preceded it. No light whatever could be thrown upon the event and no rational man for a moment supposed that the Government was responsible for this cowardly elimination of their first antagonist. London asked itself who next might be struck, and since no blow fell, people again veered to the opinion that only an extraordinary coincidence had destroyed these two prominent men.

We threshed the subject to its dregs among us, I recollect, and Jack Smith it was who pointed out the amazing dilemma with which civilization now appeared to be faced.

"You are forced to grant 'the Bat,' if bat there be, is possessed of self-consciousness," he declared, "for it is nonsense to imagine these assassinations were the work of a dumb and unreasoning animal. Either it exists and knows what it's doing, or else it is all nonsense and a figment of the mind in those who saw it. Either it seems to me that a being from some other sphere than earth is responsible for these things, or else we are up against a freak of imagination, repeated, by unconscious suggestion, in the constable who heard Ashlar's death cry; or a deliberate optical illusion—an elaborate conjuring trick, a phantom thing arranged to throw men off the scent and confuse those whose business it is to get to the bottom of the business and find out the real terrestrial cause. Two famous men are struck down, and each of them represented a power for good, or evil. Both were in deadly earnest and one certainly threatened a revolution the extent of which could not be foretold. But the man, or society of men, who hated one, might, and probably did, hate the other also."

"There is no shadow of doubt that the same agency removed both under like conditions," said Bishop Blore.

"And there is not a shadow of doubt," added Strossmayer, who was present, "that the agency is one with the destroyer of the monument."

Medland, however, stood out for his vampire, and, to my surprise, I found that General Fordyce now agreed with him.

"I still believe the choice of victims was a coincidence, and that these things are the work of a dragon, a huge, venomous reptile which has survived past ages under conditions perfectly natural if we understood them," he declared. "We know the toad will exist in entombment for centuries; why, then, should his vitality be denied to greater creatures, or limited in its duration?"

We were all interested to learn Paul Strossmayer's views, but he made no secret of them. Most firmly he believed in a human agency.

"I am only disappointed that certain unknown people have got the start of Jugo-Slavia," he said. "If this force, for that is all I will call it, is going to apply itself actively on the side of Capital against Labor's gathering powers of dictation, so much the better for civilization at large, and so much the better for this country, where the danger appears to be greatest. And whether it is human as I steadfastly believe, or super-human, as Smith suggests, so long as it is sound on economics, we shall not quarrel with its operations. If it helps the world to see that wealth is at the root of national prosperity, so much the better. One would think that the fact had been made apparent to the deaf and blind during the past two years; but the power now apparently interested in the question may do much to throw light. On the other hand, the unknown may be after something quite different that only time will reveal. It is at this moment apparently doing what I envy it the power to do; but we cannot predict the line of thought behind it, or guess how those who direct it design to proceed. Ian Noble, my young chemist with genius, is asking himself the next step and wondering if it may presently be in our power, through our own work, which is advancing swiftly, to get in touch with it."

"What do you think, Sir Bruce?" I inquired, for the general's brother had committed himself as yet to no theory of the problem.

Tonight, however, he did so, though his idea failed to convince us. He took a view, as one might have expected, based on rational opinion. The old Indian discoursed of the poison of serpents and the immense difficulties opposed to Science in its study of these subtle essences.

"I do not deny, or affirm," he added after an exposition on the physical effects seen in the two dead men. "I do not say that it was not a living creature beyond our experience, though in that case I should certainly imagine it terrestrial—a survival possibly liberated by some upheaval, or earthquake, or fluvial denudation in central Africa or America."

"In that case how would it withstand the rigors of our winter climate for a week?" asked Bishop Blore.

"It might not, Bishop. The suggestion lessens the probability of a tropical or subtropical visitant; but there are vast temperate regions of which we know little also. The creature might not be equatorial, but polar."

"You believe in it, then?" asked Medland, well pleased to win a scientific supporter of distinction. But he was disappointed.

"Most emphatically I do not believe in it," replied Sir Bruce. "The idea strains credulity too painfully. I incline to a far more prosaic opinion. I suspect these men have suffered at the hands of their fellow men, and I suppose, therefore, the apparition of 'the Bat' to be a very real and material one. In a word I should suspect an airplane, or something of that kind, either actually controlled and operated by man, or embodying some new knowledge, obedient to new powers and capable of doing its work, though the actual agents may be miles away."

"A theory distinctly more improbable than the other," declared the general. "No, no, Bruce, that really won't do. You let your scientific imagination run away with you."

Paul Strossmayer, however, supported the learned man. He had already advanced the same view, and many people found in it the only possible explanation consonant with reason. Before he spoke, however, Jacobs argued for a still more immaterial explanation and repeated his opinion that the image of the monster had never been real at all.

"How do you account for the smell then?" asked Bishop Blore. "There is no shadow of doubt about the smell. Even grant the monster a shadow, or a subconscious suggestion handed from the first policeman, at Skeat's death, to the second, who discovered Ashlar, there still remains the vulpine stench, such as Sir Bruce has admitted might belong to some order of flying mammals."

"A bat—yes; but not a reptile," interrupted Sir Bruce. "The smell is that of a warm-blooded creature, whose duration of life must be limited so far as we know. A snake, or flying saurian would not emit any such odor, if we judge by existing reptilia."

"Well, bat or lizard, the smell was reported by four men on the first occasion and three on the second. The smell cannot have been imagination and cannot have been produced by anything but a living animal."

"Your argument is worthless," returned Sir Bruce, "for smell is purely a chemical question and means the liberation of certain gases and emanations. We can imitate all odors—sweet or foul—in the laboratory."

"And what is more," struck in Strossmayer, "we are in no position to speak with authority about this effluvium, seeing we are ignorant of the energy that produced it. How many noses had ever come in contact with the smell of petrol till the advent of the motor car? That this overpowering odor accidentally resembles a smell we associate with animal life is nothing at all. Do not your people humorously describe all chemistry as the making of 'stinks'?"

He waived this minor problem from us with his long hands as a thing of no practical account and resumed, his eyes on Sir Bruce.

"Granted an airplane," he said." What follows? Much more must certainly be granted, for if a mechanical flying vessel of some kind, then it is guided, controlled and driven by a force of which as yet no human record exists."

"Do you suggest a visitor from another planet?" asked Bishop Blore.

"No, no; I only assert that no record exists. How do we know what is happening in the laboratories of Europe, or America? We only know that since the Great War every eye is opened, that visitors and vanquished alike are straining along the road and exhausting every nerve to discover secrets, which will not only ensure their own security for the future, but leave the rest of the world at their mercy."

"That may actually have been done," said Jacobs.

"It has been done—up to a point," admitted Strossmayer. "The achievement may even be complete. At any rate there exists in some human hands a power far superior to any that is common possession. The forces which have destroyed your Albert Memorial must be terrific; and the manner of that operation shows they are perfectly under control. Nothing that we know of explosives can explain the business-like and absolute destruction recorded there, or the tight hand kept on the tremendous powers responsible for it. The new energy is already being exploited, as I think, not by a nation, but a community, or society of private individuals. And since its activities take place here, we may assume that Englishmen are involved."

"A very great assumption," answered General Fordyce. "Seeing that the alien is welcome here as in no other country, and enjoys our own liberties once his foot is on our shores, we may imagine that those responsible for the discovery would naturally turn to England as the most promising country in which to pursue their initial experiments. Nor do I, for one, quarrel with them so far, seeing what form their experiments have taken. For it is certain that no Bolshevists have the secret, otherwise they would have already applied it to very different purposes."

"True," admitted Jack Smith. "They would have destroyed the Houses of Parliament rather than an object only offensive from an artistic standpoint, and they would not have smudged out Skeat, or Ashlar, but the King of England and the Prince of Wales."

"There is comfort in the thought that good conservatives may have the secret," confessed Merrivale Medland, "though, for my part, nothing I have yet heard lessens my conviction that I am right."

"In any case," I added, "it is less terrible to believe that men, like ourselves, are responsible, than to suppose that beings outside our knowledge have entered our atmosphere from another world, and are assaulting us from an angle of vision and a basis of opinion concerning which we know nothing."

"The absurdity of such an idea defeats it," declared Jacobs. "Conscious beings from another planet would hardly arrive here to quarrel about the parish pump and 'take sides' in our industrial squabbles."

"We naturally fly from contemplation of any attack directed against us by beings from another world," said Sir Bruce. "One has only to mention the possibility to see how human nature shudders at it. The idea of being approached by conscious creatures—differing from ourselves as much as we differ from familiar, unconscious creatures—plunges us into a train of thought that must be horrible in the measure of our own imagination. Suppose, for example, that some marine order of crustaceans developed the power to think and determined to invade the land and destroy our civilization and ourselves in order that they might substitute what they conceived was better; can anything more fearful than such an encounter be imagined? They would turn their submarine resources upon us and attack us with weapons of which we should have no idea until they were employed; while we should retaliate and seek to make the sea uninhabitable for them. Peace, until one side had exterminated the other, seems unthinkable, for this reason: that we should have no means of intercommunication. We might as easily imagine making a truce with a tiger, or other savage animal, as suppose that we could come to an understanding with these super-lobsters from the depth of ocean."

The gruesome idea was elaborated, and Jacobs stoutly opposed Sir Bruce's assumption that no agreement would be within reach. "Granted the possession of intellect," he said, "then, surely, a viable media might be attained? Even now we have considered the possibility of signaling to Mars, by huge symbols, which would indicate to that planet's inhabitants how conscious beings dwell in this one. Surely, therefore, if we were confronted with self-conscious crustaceans, or any other order of living creatures, it should not be beyond our power, or theirs, to establish some code, or system of signs to understanding."

"As we do when faced with tribes of savages," I added.

It was then that this somewhat unprofitable conversation ceased before a revelation, which came to us in the shape of the last edition of *The Pall Mall Gazette.*

John Linklater brought it with him from London. He was a rare visitor to the club, though popular enough when he cared to appear. His work was that of a reporter in the House of Commons. He looked in now on his way home with a startling item of intelligence.

"The murder's out," he said, handing Medland his newspaper. "Or rather both murders are out. 'The Bat' is a reality and very much alive indeed. Here's chapter and verse for the whole story, and we must look out for squalls, since the gentleman is still at large."

Chapter VI

To Save Jugo-Slavia

It was reported that a seaman from Africa—a middle-aged foreigner, who had worked with an expedition in the forest areas of the equatorial hinterland—had brought the murderous animal back to Europe with him as a cub; that, on being secured, it was no larger than a flying fox; that it had grown enormously in captivity and finally escaped.

A portrait of Joan Silva appeared in an illustrated paper next morning, with a circumstantial account of his discovery, and his own picturesque career. He was a dago from a Spanish tramp steamer, and he asserted that the place of "the Bat's" captivity had been Rosas. He was about to approach scientific authorities and invite them to take charge of his find, when it broke the iron bars of a stout cage and disappeared by night. He offered remarkable particulars of his original capture, and was ready with all details and apt answers to the questions addressed to him by Science; but, as time passed, and "the Bat" was neither seen again nor reported. Joan Silva's story began to have grave shadows cast upon it.

A skeptical journal took the matter in hand and the course of its investigations reminded the last generation of a famous and ingenious gentleman whose narrative of adventures in Australia, gulled not only the public but the intelligence of the British Association. Joan, indeed, turned out to be of the order of Louis de Rougemont and Ananias. The mariner proved himself rich in imagination and for a while his story held together and defied unfriendly criticism; but, little by little, under remorseless cross-examination, the weak spots grew larger. He could produce no witnesses and no confirmatory reports of his operations in central Africa; while the opposition was able to find a man or two who had sailed with Silva and told odd stories concerning him. He began to contradict himself and get into difficulties. He bluffed valiantly but had not the iron memory vital to successful lying; and within a month that happened to convict him of probable falsehood. Medical men proved, at any rate to their own satisfaction, that he was weak in his head, and suffered from an innocent sort of megalomania, which made him seek to challenge a wider attention than the ordinary man before the mast could hope to win. His messmates confirmed the diagnosis, and scarcely had poor Silva disappeared in a hurricane of laughter, directed more against those who had believed him than himself, when "the Bat" was again in people's minds and added very definitely to the world's knowledge of its powers. For purpose was now revealed and the certainty that it operated with full consciousness of its actions.

Time passed, spring returned and the endless business of settling the world into the ways of peace still occupied mankind and his leagues and conferences. Then, amid half a dozen other international complications, there happened a clash and confusion of interests that directly interested the Club of Friends; because strange events, arising from this conflict, offered fresh evidence and renewed grounds of suspicion against Paul Strossmayer.

His nation was directly involved in tribulation, for the politics of the little kingdom were running awry and Europe, instead of speaking with no uncertain voice, permitted Jugo-Slavia to be inflicted by a sort of comic-opera assault and looked on while a section of her neighbors, under a romantic adventurer, persisted in offensive operations having for their object the annexation of a city and the appropriation of a port. The difficulties appeared endless, and the national hero responsible for them made it hard to determine the boundaries between Jugo-Slavia and a greater nation. The Government of the ancient power desired to offer the new State all assistance; but a large and belligerent body had followed the banner of the famous artist-dictator now opposed to Jugo-Slavia. He was an aviator, celebrated during the war for his achievements against Austria, and, before it, for his magnificent orchestral compositions. Lorenzo Poglaici disputed Jugo-Slavia's rights and declined to abandon certain territory, which represented great natural wealth and stood, not only for national honor, but also for the way to the sea.

Strossmayer took a dark view of the situation and did not hesitate to declare that Poglaici's nation was in reality behind him, though it pretended to be otherwise. He proved to the satisfaction of most of us that Jugo-Slavia was right, the famous musician and his following wrong. We shared a measure of his indignation that the Entente remained dumb. And then our new member found the call of his people imperative and returned to Jugo-Slavia before the existing difficulties were composed.

The tangle was most complete and offered little hope of solution at this time; yet Strossmayer had not been in his native land a week when all changed and a grotesque situation became relieved by the sudden fate which overtook Lorenzo Poglaici himself. Flying by night above the city and territory he had appropriated in the name of his nation, this famous and picturesque being met his death. It was supposed that he had crashed, and that the hero of a thousand achievements in midair had at last suffered the too familiar fate of hundreds as bold and skillful as himself; but investigation proved the contrary and enabled Science to determine that the great man had perished aloft by means identical with those that destroyed Skeat and Ashlar in England. Thousands pictured the conflict under the stars at an elevation unguessed, and thousands were confident that Poglaici had given a good account of himself and might be counted upon to have fought to a finish and wounded or slain his awful antagonist, if given any opportunity to do so; but evidence of harm to "the Bat" was not forthcoming and whether it also had received a fatal wound and fallen to perish on land or sea, none could say. As for the dead man, it was clear that his own death and no other cause had brought his monoplane to earth. Wounds, now familiar, had robbed him of life, and it was certain that he had perished aloft and only crashed at a much lower elevation, when his machine nose-dived and came to earth headfirst.

The aviator had apparently been stabbed twice—in the breast and thigh; but there was no more to be learned from his end, and the light it threw upon the forces responsible for the tragedy was implicit rather than direct.

Men mourned the musician and artist; but were not sorry that the mistaken patriot and his aggressive personality had disappeared. They gave Lorenzo Poglaici a national funeral, and his own Government, relieved of his influence and magnetic powers, controlled his adherents and quickly settled the questions at difference in Jugo-Slavia's favor.

Paul Strossmayer, who returned to England a week after his famous enemy's destruction, made no attempt to conceal immense satisfaction at the sudden turn of affairs. Poglaici's death gave him keen gratification, while he declared himself to be wholly ignorant of the invisible and unknown forces brought into operation for this purpose.

"I neither know what slew him, or who directed the assassination," he assured us. "But this I know—that he found himself opposed by one who was stronger, swifter and far better equipped than himself. And those who reported that Poglaici was unarmed were mistaken. I myself was among those who saw him and examined his machine on the morning after his death. The error arose from finding no weapon where he fell; but subsequent search over the ground discovered a revolver of which four barrels had been discharged. That it was a presentation weapon and belonged to the dead man many, who had already seen it, were able to testify."

"He put up a fight, then?" asked Medland.

"Certainly he did."

"Yet the creature got to close quarters somehow and stabbed him as its other victims were stabbed."

"It pleases you still to imagine some aerial monster," answered Strossmayer, "but surely no intelligent man can longer hold to that."

"Be it what is is, Jugo-Slavia owes it a debt of thanks," suggested Leon Jacobs and the other agreed.

"I should be only too glad if it lay in our power to repay that debt," he replied. "The new energy has been so far exerted in a manner that all who trust to constitutional government must applaud. This last manifestation was a very timely one—both for us and Poglaici's own country. His death promises to dissolve our difficulties and their embarrassments."

"The terrific thing is this," said Jack Smith. "It is now proved to the satisfaction, or dissatisfaction, of Europe, that a shrewd and powerful intelligence is critically watching human affairs and world movements. One must, I suppose, dismiss the idea that this intelligence comes from anywhere but the earth itself; but, in any case, its intellect can appreciate events, and it has channels of ordinary knowledge like the rest of us. A living thing from another planet could only know all that this destructive force knows by communion with mankind; and seeing its line of direct action is in a sense orderly and consistent and conservative, then it follows that there need be no secrecy, for if it were proclaimed and discovered, it could still count upon a very large measure of approval and support."

"That is so," admitted Bishop Blore, "and while, ethically, all direct action of a minority, whatever its opinions, is abominable, yet there can be no doubt that in these cases the energy, or whatever you like to call it, has acted in a manner many might approve, and destroyed the activities of certain other energies represented by men, who were viewed with large distrust and dislike."

Strossmayer heartily concurred. "Those who think as we do must grant the force has been applied in no sense malignantly," he declared. "Whatever the intelligence behind it, these events prove that it is a superior intelligence, cautious, restrained and averse to any extremes of thought."

Sir Bruce, who seldom agreed with the Jugo-Slav, conceded the value of this argument.

"I, for myself, agree with you," he said. "Not long since I and those who think with me, listened with astonishment and grief to a lecture delivered before the Society of Synthetic Dyers in this country. One anticipated a peaceful and encouraging harangue, devoted entirely to progress and the advancement of industrial prosperity. But what did we hear? That the war was based on German chemistry; and that only our shameful backwardness in science prevented the recent awful conflict from being over in three months. The speaker warned his audience that the next war would depend entirely on toxic substances and that the nation most richly endowed with toxic substances would win it. We went for expert advice upon the means to advance human welfare, not warfare; instead we learned that future prosperity depends on poison gas, and are directed to devote our genius to its perfection."

"How does that bear upon the unknown?" asked Strossmayer.

"The unknown," answered Sir Bruce, "has that which banishes these foul ambitions and renders them of no account. And if this secret power can prove to civilization that it is actuated by the highest and noblest motives, as we may venture still to hope, then humanity as a whole must recognize in it a savior and not a destroyer."

"You are on the side of 'the Bat' then, Sir Bruce?" I asked; but he relapsed into his customary silence and left us to pursue the subject.

"The grand fact seems to be this," said Jacobs, "that, for good or ill, the control of the world lies on a new plane. For the first time in our history, our teachers and masters are men of science, not philosophers, clerics, or metaphysicians. Science has got the whip hand, and it remains to be seen whether it will prove a humane and beneficent autocrat, or a worse tyrant than the world has yet known."

"One would give much to learn the opinions and intentions of those who have obtained this dominion," added Bishop Blore. "They may be philosophers as well as chemists, Jacobs. They may be men inspired by our highest rules of conduct and possessed of the noblest ideals. And yet one is bound to doubt that before what has already been done; for wise men would be aware that great human movements and the aspiration of millions, but recently lifted by education out of dumb endurance, cannot be swept away with the extinction of a few individuals. The death of leaders will often serve to elevate them into martyrs, and advance, rather than retard, the causes for which they fought."

"Very true," said Jack Smith. "The battle for freedom will continue, and I much doubt whether men of science are in the least competent to take the place of our old teachers and traditional guides. Science has had to fight too long. It would not come into power without a leaven of bitterness in heart and head. Truth is many sided and there are aspects of living truth that Science cannot reconcile with reason and is too apt to undervalue."

Paul Strossmayer argued against this opinion, declaring that pure reason and the pursuit of truth qualified men of science to guide the affairs of mankind in a way they had never yet been guided; but I think most of us agreed that the lawyer had the best of it. The matter was left an open question as usual; then, some six weeks later another extraordinary manifestation of power applied against a harmless institution gave substance to Smith's argument and seemed to indicate that "the Bat," as most people still preferred to call the unknown energy, was capable of action that possessed no explanation on any human basis of reason, or unreason.

One speaks of "an institution" and, indeed, the flourishing enterprise now wiped out of existence had become such. The theater as a general term is, of course, an institution, but the entertainment at that time filling the King's Theater had specially earned the appellation; for a spectacular play was running there, and had been running to crowded and enthusiastic audiences, for the term of three years. There seemed no end to the success of "Indian Chutnee"—a massive and brilliantly mounted spectacle of the East, which depended upon the splendor of its production, the magic of the dresses and the beauty of the music for its achievement, rather than any coherent or dramatic theme. But in a night the King's was wiped out of existence.

Moving along a line of former activity the unknown forces attacked bricks and mortar, and at a time when the great building was empty, liberated such a volume of energy upon it that the theater and all it contained was turned to a mountain of dust. Again the force was exquisitely controlled, and despite its immensity, nothing but the doomed house of entertainment suffered. The intelligence behind this weapon would kill a fly as deftly as it could crush a cathedral. And here again, by the attitude he took upon this new manifestation, our foreign member once more gave his detractors an opportunity. Fate seemed to will that, by word or deed, he should be linked in varying degrees of probability with the unknown. That he was in Jugo-Slavia when Lorenzo Poglaici perished appeared proof positive to certain minds, easily made up and already tinged with prejudice against him; but in the affair of the theater, the opinion he expressed could hardly be regarded with any justice as inspired by secret knowledge. Indeed one other, who certainly knew nothing of the matter, had arrived at the same conclusion independently.

Bishop Blore, who appeared to take a benevolent interest in "the Bat," and while deploring its actions, argued that they might spring from high motives, was considering this last occurrence, which he declared had gone far to weaken his hopes.

None, of course, further questioned the certainty that all the unexplained events proceeded from the same source, since chemistry had proved the connection. The Bishop, therefore, spoke under the general assumption.

"This last outrage shakes me," he confessed, "for even if we condone what is past, how are we to forgive an act that robs the world of innocent enjoyment and throws five hundred people out of work? No theory of decent conduct, no far-reaching design for the increased happiness of the world, can fit with this insensate act. Nor, am I told, was there anything to annoy anybody in the performance. I never go to the theater and am not in a position to judge, but Jacobs assures me the production was devoid of offence, and only a fanatical objection to all theatrical performances could explain such an action."

"It seems isolated," said I. "It does not fit in with anything that has gone before. There is nothing in common between this assault and the destruction of the Albert Memorial. One cannot explain it on any human values."

Already our company began to grow thin, for not a few members of the Club of Friends were about the business of their annual holiday; but Paul Strossmayer happened to be there on this occasion, and it was he who answered me.

"I believe you are absolutely right, Granger," he replied. "And what follows? Surely we may agree as to the only possible explanation. Conscious intelligence is, of course, at work, not blind force hurled out of an indifferent sky; but all humanity must be fallible, and, in a word, I believe those who are running this secret of radioactive energy have made a mistake. They are men like ourselves, and on the night when chance destroyed the King's

Theater, somebody blundered. Let us endeavor to find what goes on in the buildings which surround the theater; then we may perhaps judge better of the intended target."

He spoke so positively, that neither the bishop nor anybody else was prepared to contradict him. Indeed Bishop Blore accepted this conclusion with considerable satisfaction.

"For the credit of mankind, I hope you are right," he said, "and since I am always quick to accept any thing to the credit of our noble selves, I will believe that you are right. The explanation is reasonable, though one longs for details and proof that the object of attack was worthy of attack. Indeed there are few things I desire more keenly nowadays than the explanation of these mysteries. They absorb me. I find my mind preoccupied with them at all manner of inappropriate times. Humanity seems to be on the very verge of some astounding increase of knowledge and, if I have a quarrel with the unknown, it is because this addition to our stock of wisdom is hidden from the race of men. For that no excuse exists."

"When the time comes, they will have to face an insulted world and explain themselves; though it will be difficult," said Medland. "But we may be on a wrong track as I told you before. Coincidence plays a large part in life, and these events, whatever Science may be pleased to think, may yet be proved to spring from different causes for which Science is not responsible." He still clung to his own theory; and time was to prove that, after all, phenomena outside any human knowledge would again intrude upon men's minds.

For the present I am only concerned to state that Strossmayer's suggestion of an accident was partially accepted; but even those who did not doubt that he must be right, judged him adversely upon it, and believed he spoke from inner knowledge denied to the majority of mankind. Indeed Jack Smith voiced others as well as himself when he hinted as much.

A veiled antagonism already existed between them, and their arguments, not on this subject alone, but others, embracing the code of laws on which Jugo-Slavia was to be conducted, often approached acrimony.

"You know so much, Mr. Strossmayer, that perhaps you know more," said Smith bluntly on this occasion.

"It is your mistaken opinion that I do, and I wish you were right," replied the other warmly and swift to pick up the challenge. "Nothing would afford me greater satisfaction than to declare your constant insinuations were just. If I possessed the secret, it might even give me a little pleasure to offer you practical illustration and proof that I did! Meantime, you, and not only you, continue to entertain the opinion that I lie. But why certain members of this club imagine that I know more of these astounding events than they do, or that I am, so to speak, behind the scenes in the matter, I cannot guess."

"I will tell you, then," answered the lawyer. "You, yourself, are to blame, for you admit that you and your friends in this country, or perhaps I should say your friend—the chemist, Ian Noble—are deeper in the mystery of radioactive elements than anybody else. You have openly declared that you are on the track of the unknown energy."

"What of it?" asked the other. "To be on the track of the energy is not to be on the track of those who are now employing it. We may be nearer to these people than you are; we may presently even discover them, by first discovering the means which they employ; but we are no nearer to understanding their purposes, or measuring their intentions, than yourself. Be reasonable and consider what I gain by the things that are being done."

"That is a question easily answered," replied Smith. "What you gained by the death of Skeat, for example, seems clear. He insulted you here before us all, and you might well have taken means to punish him by death, seeing that in the eyes of your nation an insult demands to be answered, if need be, with blood. Every country has its own code of honor, and I should not blame you if your code demanded a more tremendous retort in such a case than my own. But let that pass. You are out for Jugo-Slavia, first, last and always. Again I do not blame you. But look at facts. You knew that Lorenzo Poglaici was a thorn in the flesh of your people, and doing far greater damage, by his mischievous and romantic nonsense, than sane men could quickly or easily remedy. Obviously you and yours all stood to gain by his removal. And you go to Jugo-Slavia and he is removed. Is it then unreasonable to argue that cause and effect are here apparent? You resent our suspicions; but you cannot deny that they are at least grounded on a pretty solid basis."

The other considered before replying. He was not annoyed any longer; but evidently astonished. An element of something almost akin to amusement entered into his expression as he frankly regarded Jack Smith.

His answer turned away wrath. "I stand corrected," he replied. "I swear to you with all my heart and soul, before the God I recognize, that I have had no hand in these things; but I no longer ask you, or any of your friends, to believe me if you consider such an oath upon my lips insignificant. It is true what you say. Had I been such a man and possessed such a power, I might have used it upon Alexander Skeat, who wounded me with his brutality; and, again, for my country's good, I might willingly have destroyed my country's enemy. I will go further and confess I should not have hesitated to do so. I rejoice that it was done, and a step gained thereby to the universal peace for which we groan. But I did neither of these things, because, though I am now sanguine that I shall live to see the new energy won for Jugo-Slavia, as yet it is not won, at any rate by us."

Smith bowed, but declined to leave the difference composed; then Jacobs unfortunately struck in. There was little love lost at any time between him and the lawyer, and now he took Smith to task somewhat sharply.

"Surely," he said, "when a man goes so far and answers your baseless suspicions with such good temper and patience, it becomes you, for the credit of your own race, to be decent and conciliatory."

But Jack Smith resented his interference and stabbed Leon before he left the room. "East will cling to East, of course," he said. "You are like most alien people who dwell in England, Jacobs. England is only a place to get a good living out of, not a country to love. You have no real kinship with the West; at heart you would rather be against us than with us. You know, as well as I do, the truth of what I say."

He was gone before Jacobs had time to reply. Indeed he attempted no reply. The insult really seemed too absurd even to acknowledge, for no more patriotic English Jew than my friend existed. He had been bred and educated in England and, while proud of his own historic nationality, was British in most of his opinions. Unlike many of his race, who have attained to distinction and honor among us, he respected his foster country and had always done so.

I hastened to lessen the sting of this egregious attack by boldly hinting that Smith must be the worse for his usual "nightcap," and by assuring Leon that the man would tender him an apology for such insolence at the first opportunity.

I then turned to Strossmayer, changed the subject, and reminded him of a former promise. He appreciated the championship of Jacobs and radiantly granted my request.

"When are we to see your prodigy—the radio-chemist?" I asked. "He was to have paid us a visit and given us a glimpse into the new chemistry, upon which the future seems so directly to depend."

"He shall come," replied the other. "I am anxious for him to do so; but I hesitated to bring him under the growing weight of opinion directed against me here. I say nothing, but have been aware for some time that I was not *persona grata* save in certain quarters. However, I can easily leave you and, indeed, shall do so before long. But I will bring Ian Noble when he returns to England. For the moment he is in Vienna and proceeds to Belgrade to see my Government next week. On his return he shall come."

Strossmayer kept his word; but the installation of certain apparatus and the consideration of plans for new laboratories projected in his future home kept Noble out of England for several weeks, and when he did visit Chislehurst, to accept the hospitality of the Club of Friends, there were but few members left to welcome him. Our little coterie was on the wing for the summer, and among those who had already departed were General Hugh Fordyce and his brother, Sir Bruce, who had gone to the latter's estate in Devonshire. Merrivale Medland was off, as usual, to combine business with pleasure in France and Spain, and he, too, missed the visitor; while Jack Smith departed on a walking tour, but made no attempt to patch his quarrel before doing so.

Chapter VII

The New Chemistry

It was on an evening in July when Ian Noble actually visited us; and despite his youth, one could not fail to be conscious of a personality. For a young man he was remarkably sedate. Alert and alive he indeed seemed to be, but there appeared in him none of the exuberant quality of youthful genius. He did not assert himself, and let us appreciate his quality as much by his silences as through what he said. He was a Scot of dark complexion and lean, wiry build. His age was nine and twenty, but his clean-shorn face, thin jaw and lined forehead made him look ten years older. His life of toil had aged him, yet detracted nothing from a native frankness and urbanity of temper. He made no mistake about his own capabilities, or the vital importance of the work upon which he was engaged at this time; but he was not pretentious and he appeared to belong to that distinguished order of scientific inquirers who labor for the sake of truth, rather than to advance their fame, or improve their worldly position. He was, in fact, modest and far more interested with general questions embracing the future prospects of science, in its relations to humanity, than in his personal achievements and contributions to knowledge. He echoed Strossmayer, that to Science must the world look for its future salvation, and he argued that the spirit of Science was misunderstood.

"Our stern and unyielding respect for truth is regarded by some minds as almost brutal," he declared. "I find people who actually seem to think all research is based on infliction of suffering! It is monstrous. They forget that the principal sufferers are the scientists themselves and the amount of suffering that Science has already saved the world."

Concerning his own activities he would say very little, and while he made the line of his inquiry clear, he vouchsafed no light on the extent of his success, or where he now stood with reference to the great goal. He was not secretive, but diffident, and Strossmayer had more to say on that point than the chemist. Noble was a water-drinker and did not smoke; but he had a good appetite and enjoyed his dinner. He liked to talk when conscious of sympathetic auditors, and after we had adjourned to the smoking room, Paul Strossmayer soon launched him into his favorite, though by no means his only, theme.

"The time has long passed," he said, "since our immortal Boyle declared that we could pursue the secret of matter into the elements and no further. The elements themselves have increased in number since his day, and such modern chemists as Becquerel and the Curies have atomized these elements. The atom is the starting point of modern chemistry, and from it we reach radioactivity and so proceed to the hidden mysteries of transmutation. They are no mysteries really: there is no such thing as a mystery in our domain; but for the present they continue to remain hidden from our intelligence, though time will surely yield the key to the door that still hides them."

"The circle seems to complete itself," said Bishop Blore, "and I read that you latest seekers may yet show us that the inquiries of the old alchemists had something in them, after all. In my youth we were taught that the philosopher's stone and the elixir of life were moonshine."

"Far from it," answered Noble. "Transmutation is proved; but the ancient road would never have led to that discovery. Transmutation, I say again, is proved, and homogeneity, or identity, becomes a delusion of past scientists when we find elemental atoms composed of materials fundamentally different. For, pushed to its conclusion, this fact may reveal that the same element will transmute iron, or lead, or gold."

"How push it to its conclusion?" asked Jacobs.

"That is the present puzzle," admitted the young chemist. "That we cannot do yet, and to the bedrock, we may, of course, never actually get. But, on the other hand, we may; and, though my opinion is of little worth, I think we shall."

"We can control chemical changes easily enough," explained Strossmayer. "That is one thing; but to control the changes of the atom is quite another."

"Quite another," echoed Ian Noble. "We cannot make the atom expel a particle if it declines to do so, or retain a particle, if it is determined to expel it. Take radium. Radium will not retain its particles for anybody; while lead will not expel them. Wild horses won't make lead expel a particle. As yet we know not how to do so; but if lead would only oblige in this little matter, we might turn it into gold at will, by way of mercury and thallium."

"That, then, is the secret lying between us and the philosopher's stone?" asked the bishop. "Exactly—no more and no less," answered Noble. "But there is another and far more tremendous consideration. The energy implied by 'the Bat,' though as yet unknown to the world at large, is now in human hands; and those who reached it, only did so by discovering the way to the whole secret."

"Do you mean?" I inquired, "that those responsible for these extraordinary murders and destructions have the power to turn lead into gold?"

"In all probability they have," he assured us. "One cannot be positive, and one heartily hopes that the full, potential limit still lies beyond their reach—for this reason. If we learn how to turn lead into gold, we learn a much more terrific fact: we learn to control and release atomic energy—such energy as might split the solid rind of the earth, like a cocoanut under a steam hammer."

"Do you mean that man will ever be in a position to destroy the world?" asked Bishop Blore with amazement on his face.

"I do," answered the young man calmly. "That is what we shall most certainly be able to achieve, when we find out how to transmute the elements."

"An appalling prospect," confessed Leon Jacobs; "for put a case. Such a discovery would argue genius of the very highest order—an amazing intellect—and such a brain, rewarded perhaps by this awful discovery after a lifetime of gigantic toil, might well totter on the brink of insanity. Imagine such a power in the hand of a lunatic and our very cosmical existence is not worth a day's purchase!"

Noble nodded.

"That is the truth—an appalling prospect, as you say; and what is more, for certain reasons and from the evidence before us of the unknown's activities, your gloomy suggestion may be nearer the truth than you suppose."

But Bishop Blore raised his voice in protest. "You leave the Maker of the round world out of your calculations," he assured our guest. "Shall the Almighty suffer His planet to be at the mercy of a creature? Shall we permit one of afflicted mind to exterminate the earth, as a lunatic destroys some harmless man, or child?"

But Jacobs perceived that the good prelate had given himself into a rationalist's hand.

"That is dangerous ground, Bishop," he replied, "for the evils you suggest, which we know have too often happened, only differ in magnitude from what we imagine. If it is denied that a madman may extinguish a world, why is it allowed that he may take an innocent life?"

Paul Strossmayer brought us back to the subject. "Since you suspect such colossal perils, my friend," he said to Noble, "the quicker you find an antidote and give our 'Bat' a dose of his own physic, the better for Jugo-Slavia."

But the other only broke off from his lecture to chaff.

"All very well, Paul; but remember I am not the man to be enslaved for a party, or a State. I had to make that mighty clear when I was in your very attractive country, and among your very attractive countrymen. You are a most astute person—everybody in Jugo-Slavia appears to be astute for that matter—but with a sort of astuteness that made me kick a little. You, yourself, are as honest as the light; but your people are—what? Shall we say, 'self-centered'? You must not keep us chemists on a chain, to bark for Jugo-Slavia alone. You must not exploit us, Paul."

"Why use the word?" asked Strossmayer. "You know very well, Noble, that your first duty is to your employer, and though you discover something of worldwide significance, as you will, your first duty is still to your employer. You have accepted our general terms, and if we like to keep a menagerie of scientists in luxury and affluence, on the off chance that the game is worth the candle, that is our affair. But it is your affair to give us your results be they great or small—be they only to make two ears of corn grow where one has grown, or split the world like a nut, as you say."

"Granted," answered his friend. "We will talk of that another time, when there is something to talk about. I shall not be found lacking in enthusiasm for Jugo-Slavia which has treated me so well, is building me the finest laboratory in Europe, and not denying me the most costly materials for research within human reach. All that I fully recognize. The means to wealth and the power which arises out of wealth, if I discover them, are Jugo-Slavia's; but the application to which those means shall be put—have I no voice in that vital matter?"

"We will talk of this another time, as you suggested," replied the other. "This is a personal question and cannot interest our friends."

The younger man, showing a trace of discomposure, was silent a few moments; then he dismissed that aspect of his activities and turned to us.

"If you want research, you must go outside the Universities," he said. "University professors are paid to teach, not to learn, and many a creative man is smothered in a Chair. State departments are chiefly concerned to prop up the old, not to foster the new; and law, officialdom, the Constitution itself, have always supported the noncreative, selfish interests of mankind. Nevertheless Science is winning a place in the sun at last. This argues no particular good will on the part of our rulers, but only a general, though still foggy, perception that the future prosperity of civilization depends upon Science. The Arts need not be afraid, for as our claim is universal, so are our obligations. Science is acutely aware of its obligations and perceives their immensity, when it shall reach these gigantic powers presently to be discovered."

"They must be applied to the boon, not the bane, of humanity," asserted Bishop Blore, and none differed from his pious hope.

"That is every good man's wish," answered Noble, "but Science is clear-eyed and appreciates the complexity of the problem. The quest itself is difficult enough and success may be long delayed; but consider how far more difficult will be what follows discovery. The problem of applying our mighty energy to the good of all men and the advancement of the whole world's progress, will be one calling for a vaster intellect than is yet upon this earth. Indeed no solitary brain, or nation, can be expected to administer such an inheritance impartially."

"The new energy must be the servant, not the tyrant, of man," I said.

"But how easily—how fatally easily—might it become the tyrant," he replied.

Paul Strossmayer was growing a little uneasy at this development of the theme. "Don't preach, Ian," he said abruptly. "Leave that to Bishop Blore. Give us chemical facts, not ethical theories: they are not your line." But a flush came into the chemist's pale face, though he answered quietly.

"You may find that they are," he replied. "Even a man of science must be granted a heart as well as a head, Paul; and I imagine no chemist is the worse for loving his fellow creatures and desiring to increase universal happiness. You must not deny me my enthusiasms or ideals, even though my business is concerned with the search for truth alone. Indeed where shall we find a greater or more precious truth than the right application of knowledge to the advancement of man's welfare?"

The bishop applauded this sentiment. "Wisely spoken," he declared. "Learning misapplied is worse than ignorance. When it is within our reach, let our greatest good be shared by all."

"Easy to wish, your lordship," answered the Scot; "but how inconceivably difficult to accomplish. None should know better than a prince of the Church how hard must be the task before us. Consider that we have been seeking to apply the panacea of Christianity to human affairs for nearly two thousand years, since the concept first dawned upon mankind. There you see the problem paralleled; and if moral precepts and a lofty, universal rule of conduct are so hard to establish, so apparently impossible of human application, who can assert that some immense, physical discovery, however full of promise and hope, will not prove equally difficult to set going in right channels?"

"Until we make the world safe for righteousness, we certainly shall never make it safe for unlimited energy," admitted Bishop Blore. "I must grant you that mankind has failed, so far, to employ that most glorious of all energies, the gift of the Founder of Christianity, which we call love. That He has placed at our service; He has erected its altars in every human soul; but few there are who worship at those altars with a single heart. The fault, however, lies in human weakness and fallibility, not in the gift itself."

Noble bowed respectfully.

"It is good to find a distinguished churchman honest enough to admit the failure," he answered.

Then Leon Jacobs spoke. "Great forces which might unite and pull together, still, by some unhappy, inherent weakness in us, are content to oppose their strength," he said. "If the Church had the sense to support Science and elevate the application of its discoveries into the field of morals, she might yet justify herself to many skeptic minds. But she kicks against the pricks of knowledge, and so gives herself dangerous wounds, which only lower her own vitality. She quarrels with Science, denies and grudges its discoveries, cheapens its conclusions, fights against the inevitable and resistless progress of truth and ignores all the salutary cleansing, saintly work that Science has done and is doing for the amelioration of human suffering."

"It must be so," reluctantly confessed the bishop. "No honest man can pretend a reconciliation, for reconciliation is impossible. One reads the annual sermon before the British Association and realizes the futility and hollowness of such a friendship. We have held the knife to the throat of Science too long, and Science retaliates—with no knife indeed—but by the liberation of an air so icy that Faith cannot breathe it. Let each of us, therefore, look to the order in his own house and leave the reconciliation of Faith and Science to the Everlasting."

"Faith must not be denied us, however," answered Noble. "Dogmatism is death to Science; but nonetheless we have a very deeply rooted faith, and if I gave it a name I should call it belief in the evolution of human morals and a sure trust that such evolution tends upwards, despite the darkness of the times in which we happen to live. An ephemeral insect, that lives and dies on a gray day, might deny the existence of the sun; but though our span of years may happen to be gray, reason and unconquerable hope still tell the man of science that the sun is shining, presently to emerge for generations as yet unborn."

A vivid animation characterized the young man's utterance and light seemed to shine upon his face as he spoke. Bishop Blore looked at him with a sort of regret. Indeed the elder man voiced his emotion.

"Would that your brain had developed the little extra twist, to bring you on our side," he said frankly.

"There are only two sides," answered the chemist; "and I make bold to believe I am on yours—in all things that matter."

But the old prelate shook his head.

After this excursion into morals, our guest returned to his own subject.

"Energy is the point," he explained. "There are two energies, the sleeping and waking. A loaded gun cartridge is potential energy. We may scatter the powder or dynamite on the ground and the energy is lost; but put the cartridge into your gun and fire it, then the energy becomes kinetic, active, awake. We hold that the energy that is waiting to alter the face of the earth and change her tears to smiles is close to our hands—sleeping. Everything is embraced in matter and its product, energy. All that has ever happened, or can happen, is comprehended in those words. The beings who have done these obscure deeds—men, as of course, I believe—stored energy and then liberated it. In the case of the Albert Memorial, energy was poured out, to the destruction of those earlier energies that created and erected it. Energy is being stored in secret—that is what we have to recollect. Vast energies are being bottled and locked up ready for use by unknown men; and they choose that we should grope in the dark blindly, only seeing a little at a time of their purpose."

"And we are on their track," added Strossmayer. "They are a good way ahead still; but Noble is going to catch them up and pass them presently!"

"I make no such promise," answered the other, "though I believe and, indeed, am sure, that we are upon their track, because there is only one track. They are chemists, for what they have learned could only come by that road. And they are at this moment far the greatest chemists in the world, by virtue of their achievement. Great chemists, but not great men."

"Why do you say that?" asked Paul Strossmayer.

"Because the first impulse of a true follower of Science is to enrich the world with his knowledge. These people are not in the great tradition, otherwise their secret had before now became common property. But I condemn them for more than that. They have given very stupid signs of a reactionary spirit—I speak of their murders—and how can we believe that those who have already done what they have done are in any sense worthy of the power that they control?"

Jacobs agreed with the visitor. "One can only read them in the light of their demonstrations," he declared. "Their ultimate purpose is still hidden."

After further conversation, Bishop Blore asked pointedly whether Noble had any inkling of those responsible for the recent catastrophes.

"You are informed, no doubt, of the best that is being done in your own line of inquiry," he said, "for, as you truly tell us, Science keeps no secrets, but is only concerned to publish what may add to the sum of human knowledge. Do you, therefore, suspect any school of workers, or any nation known to be busy with radioactivity? Can you point to a possible starting place for these things?"

"Emphatically no," answered our guest. "Neither I, nor any of my acquaintance and coworkers, has so much as a theory of the puzzle, let alone a clue. It beats us, both here and in Germany and in America. And we are chiefly beaten by the phenomena themselves. They may not be called irrational; but they are vague, if not contradictory. They indicate no point of view that we should expect to find displayed by any enlightened people."

"What, then, of the theory that unconscious forces are responsible?" I asked. "How should you answer the supposition that there are two energies at work?"

"I have proved that there is but one," answered Strossmayer. "My theory has been accepted so far."

"Undoubtedly there is but one energy," admitted Ian Noble.

"Then what of 'the Bat'?" inquired Bishop Blore. But the visitor declared absolute unbelief upon this point.

"I am among those who decline to accept your Bat, Bishop," he replied, little guessing the experience that awaited him in the future. "I judge 'the Bat' to belong to the region of psychoanalysis, suggestion and mental obscurity. 'The Bat' was handed on from policeman to policeman. You must look for that animal where you look for the Russians who crossed England to get to the front in France, or the angels reported from Mons."

"Strange that one accustomed, no doubt, to examine evidence so closely as yourself should reject such evidence as can be furnished for the flying monster, Mr. Noble," ventured Bishop Blore; but the young man was positive upon this point and declined to accept such proof as had been forthcoming for a living animal. Indeed he spoke with emphatic assurance, the greater by contrast with his usual guarded conversation.

And three days after his visit to us, it seemed for a season that his convictions were justified, for an amazing triple murder of a character purely political was reported from Rome. In broad day three men were suddenly destroyed, and while no doubt existed that they had perished by the same means as those recorded in connection with the alleged apparition of a strange, winged animal, on this occasion "the Bat" had not been seen at all.

Chapter VIII

Grimwood

Three unfortunate men, a Russian Jew, a Savoyard and an Italian, had almost simultaneously succumbed to the unknown power now so actively intervening in human affairs.

The Fourth Internationale was sitting at Rome, and the trio now snatched from the councils of extreme socialism had stood among its most prominent leaders. They sought with demoniac energy to destroy the existing order of society; they employed their oratory to inspire the people with their convictions, and plunge Europe into the melting pot of a ruthless revolution, that civilization might reappear, purged of every ideal and interest save those for which they stood.

Ivan Bronstein, Gerard Clos, and Vergilio Paravicini were returning side by side from a morning session through the Piazza di Spagna, and had apparently turned to ascend the great flight of steps ascending behind the fountain. It was after noon, at a moment when the piazza happened to be thinly peopled; but not a few had followed the famous men, and many independent witnesses recorded the circumstance of their destruction in bright sunshine and without visible means.

Suddenly, with his foot on the first step of the great flight, Bronstein was seen to fling up his arms and sprawl forward upon his face. His companions, suspecting the excitement of the conference had proved to great—for Ivan Bronstein was an old man—bent to succor him, probably fearing no more than a fainting fit. But, as they did so, first Paravicini and then Clos leapt to his feet, only to fall—one upon the other beside their prostrate companion. Thus, in a moment, all three had been swept from life by an invisible hand.

Spectators of the tragedy hastened forward and the victims were quickly attended; but all had perished and, to the amazement of Italy and discomfiture of their party, it became swiftly apparent that all had died by the stroke responsible in the case of other eminent men. No visible event of any kind had explained the sudden collapse; no witness of the event had heard the least explosion, or seen the anarchists accosted. They were, indeed, marked men and familiar heroes to the Roman proletariat; a thousand would have willingly died to protect them; but they were gone; the unseen power had overwhelmed them in furtherance of a steadfast policy, which now began clearly to emerge.

As though by a flash of lightning, the three great extremists were banished from the earth; but no lightning was responsible for their extinction. Postmortem examinations revealed that all had fallen by the means formerly reported. A radioactive agent had entered Bronstein through his back, Clos upon the left side of his head, Paravicini at his stomach; in death they furnished the same phenomena as those who had passed before them. A red pinprick was all that could externally be detected; the disintegration and something akin to transmutation of their elements occurred within.

The three were cremated and interred with imposing ceremonial, and Demos throughout Europe and America began to be seriously disturbed concerning the tremendous weapon now directed so methodically and remorselessly against it. Much passion was aroused and immense unrest. Class war entered the sphere of practical politics, and those best able to judge of the trend now given to a secret and subterranean movement, apprehended that any future demonstration along the lines of this triple assassination would precipitate the struggle and let loose revolution upon a weary earth striving to regain stability and equilibrium.

Danger threatened on every hand, and Labor, together with various anarchic forces that masquerade in its name, began to shout through many mouthpieces that their traditionary foes had "cornered" some terrific new power and designed its ruthless application against the people.

An opinion so grotesque needed only publication to meet the ridicule of all reasonable men; but the alarm took wing from a thousand angry tongues and in a hundred journals; it was not adequately refuted or denied and, as usual, erroneous impressions on fiery and eloquent lips seduced innumerable listeners, who found reason in temperate mouths a tame substitute for the more forcible and trenchant utterances of their own leaders.

Revolution, then, spread dark wings in the upper air, and already shadowed mankind. Incidentally the international detective forces, employed by night and day upon the problem, were for a time relieved of the phantom of "the Bat"; and yet it was not a month after these events that the mystery again appeared.

For the first time the United States of America became a theater for its activities, and thence it was reported in connection with incidents of the most amazing character.

In their order, however, I must first relate occurrences of a nature personal to the Club of Friends, for it is not without good reason that I have undertaken this record and written it, so to speak, from our club window. A time swiftly approached when our modest coterie was destined to figure largely in the world's interest and suffer a flood of light focalized upon its little company. Thus the conventional and commonplace may often emerge into a blaze of passing publicity, in virtue of extrinsic interests for which, in itself, it is not responsible.

Paul Strossmayer indeed—a passing presence, a bird of passage—was the only man among us who could be magnified into a personality, or described as a man out of the ordinary; and he continued to be a lively object of interest and contention behind his back. His detractors eagerly pointed out that he was absent from Chislehurst on the occasion of the tragedy at Rome; and he had indeed left England; but Leon Jacobs, who enjoyed the foreigner's friendship, was in a position to tell us that Strossmayer did not visit Italy at this time. He himself had seen the Jugo-Slav off upon his travels; and his destination was America. Before departing, moreover, he had explained to Jacobs that his purpose was but an extension of the quest that had brought him to this country. He had gone to New York, Chicago, and San Francisco that he might study the work of the more advanced laboratories and win, if possible, further adherents by the offer of generous inducements. In England he confessed that his search, save for brilliant exceptions, had proved disappointing; but he hoped for valuable rewards in "God's Own Country" and desired also to learn the opinion of American experts on the subject of the new energy now liberated upon earth.

"The accursed war," he told Jacobs, "has taken too heavy a toll of your young men of genius, and time must lapse, a new generation rise, before the sort of people we want are to be had for the seeking. Ian Noble is merely a survival. Had he gone to the war, doubtless he would have perished; but it so happened the Government needed him and would not let him volunteer. And now with Noble's advice and direction, I go to America, where radioactivity is at the forefront of research. He begins to suspect that it is in America that the secret has been, so far, discovered; and he has one personal friend, at Boston, whom I must secure at any cost."

Paul Strossmayer, then, was in America, or supposed to be, and Jacobs, soon after his departure, prepared for a vacation to the Swiss lakes. For me, holidays were never any great attraction, and though I took the month of August annually, I often regretted that it was not possible to hand the leisure weeks to somebody who stood more in need of change and relaxation. I had almost determined to visit Cumberland and enlarge a very limited acquaintance with my native land, when an alternative was presented and I received a letter from General Fordyce, which, after brief consideration, changed my plans. He wrote from Grimwood, South Brent, South Devon, his brother's place.

Grimwood, as I already knew, had descended to the general at his father's death, but he was a poor man and did not appreciate the country, save for a few months of shooting in the autumn. Sir Bruce, however, for sentimental reasons, connected with his dead mother and sister, chose to preserve his old home in the family, though there was none to follow him there, and he had told me, when speaking of it, that his means did not permit of keeping up Grimwood in a manner worthy of so fine an estate. I found afterwards that he made no attempt whatever to sustain the vanished splendors of his ancestral halls, and was apparently content to let the mansion go to ruin, while he occupied but half a dozen chambers in it, and that only during the summer months.

And now General Hugh invited me to join his brother rather than himself. Indeed he made a great favor of such a visit; reminded me that I was accustomed to regard my annual holiday as a nuisance rather than a pleasure, and promised me some beautiful scenery at the foothills of Dartmoor and pleasant bicycle or motor excursions to the sea and surrounding scenes of historical interest.

Thus he wrote:

> "My Dear Granger: I know that holidays are no more than a necessary hiatus in your orderly existence, and since the fatal month of August is now again threatening you with enforced idleness, I am going to suggest that you kill two birds with one stone—take your change and do me a good turn by taking it here.

"Sir Bruce is fond of you: you see eye to eye with him in many directions and he appreciates your restful company and capacity for quiet. If you could put in even a couple of weeks with him, it would give him real pleasure and reconcile him to my departure; for I am engaged to friends in Scotland and a shooting party later on at the Derbyshire Peak.

"Between ourselves, however, I shall have to deny myself these amusements if you cannot come to Grimwood, for my brother is not in his best form. It seems absurd to suggest that a man of such iron constitution, vigor, and mental and physical activity is weakening, and I do not think that his indisposition can be more than transitory; but you know what a soft heart he has got and how he hardly endures the woe of the world. Disasters weigh heavily upon his shoulders; he feels many things acutely and takes a gloomy rather than a sanguine view of the future. He was always a pessimist by temperament, and life, though it has brought him well-deserved recognition and distinction, has also inflicted upon him his share of private sorrows. He cannot change his outlook now, and my cheerful habit of saying 'yea' to life and trusting a future generation to make a better business of civilization than we have gives him no satisfaction. Indeed there is not much to be cheerful about, I grant; but, as I tell Bruce, the individual can only do his duty and leave the fate of mankind in the Hands of Him who made them.

"Do come if it is within your power; but do not think I design a martyrdom. We lie in the midst of noble scenery, within easy distance of the sea and among scenes and places of historical attraction. You will have ample freedom to enjoy these things; indeed, if you are at home for dinner and a chat with my brother afterwards, that is all I ask. He seldom breakfasts downstairs and is for the most part invisible till after noon. You will, therefore, be free as air to pursue your own amusement.

"But I know this is putting a strain on friendship and I shall perfectly understand if your plans are made and the suggestion should prove impracticable. I hope the 'Friends' are well, though doubtless most of our little company is away.

"Always sincerely yours,

"Hugh Fordyce"

I was well pleased to oblige the general, and after August Bank Holiday had passed, set off for Devonshire—a county not familiar to me. My host met me at South Brent and we drove under the Southern ranges of the great Devon tableland to Grimwood, distant five miles from the station.

The approach, after traveling through a network of interminable lanes, rendered stuffy and airless by the height of the hedges, proved somewhat imposing. We descended a long avenue of ancient elms, then entered a great cup or "coomb" of beautiful park land, upon the northern side of which, its long front facing south, stood Grimwood.

Forests surrounded the grasslands and rose densely on all sides of the park. They seemed to press forward in great hanging woods on every quarter of the compass, and threaten to flow down with floods of heavy summer green to drown the mansion and the narrow gardens of pleasure that extended before it.

The drive was mossy and neglected, and many trees showed evidence of decay. Here a winter storm had uprooted three together, but still their dead carcasses lay beside the way. As for the house, seen half a mile distant, it was dignified in design, though ruined to an architectural eye by the ivy that had been permitted to mantle its face, climb to the roofs and destroy its outlines; but, at nearer approach, I was startled, for the great front showed many evidences of decay; the battlements were broken, and a portion of the eastern face already appeared ruinous. General Fordyce observed my surprise, which I fear was not concealed as carefully as manners might have demanded.

"It's the ivy," he said. "I'm always at Bruce to strip the place and do something to it, but he is preoccupied and won't bother. His own wing is all right, though. All this end has been empty for half a century, and our damp climate is responsible for these rather melancholy results."

But Grimwood was more than melancholy in my eyes. Something brooding belonged to it. I felt a spirit in the air—a spirit of dissolution and decay, not only sorrowful but sinister. Beauty still harbored in the distinguished Elizabethan elevation; but one felt it lingered upon this mossgrown and neglected edifice only as the sunset, and promised soon to vanish.

"It will last my time," said Sir Bruce, when a week later, at his own invitation, I had expressed my opinion of his home, coupled with a fear that the fabric call for far-reaching attention.

It was a fortified manor house of two stories spreading under a long and battlemented roof—a very lonely habitation, for the nearest of the estate's five farmhouses stood a mile away, beyond the ring of forest that hemmed it in.

Upon our drive on the evening of my arrival, General Hugh thanked me very heartily for coming, and was evidently glad to be gone himself. The brothers were so different in their outlook upon life that, though close family feeling and natural affection bound them together, no tougher and more vital bonds of conviction and imagination linked their minds.

Sir Bruce welcomed me with genuine pleasure, and finding him in excellent health and spirits, I suspected that his brother's discovery of threatened illness had in reality been caused by himself. For I have known relations gravely to disturb each other and then, unconscious that the distracting element sprang from themselves, to declare a fear that the object of their solicitation was unwell. At any rate the master of Grimwood greeted me with more than friendship and repeated his satisfaction at my visit. He was glad, or good enough to say he was glad, of my companionship, while at the same time insisting on a large freedom for me. He made me take long excursions upon the moors and beside the sea; and though he often accompanied me to scenes of old-time importance or natural beauty, yet frequently expressed a wish that I should sometimes desert him and amuse myself alone.

That was not difficult to do, for his library attracted me even more than the rare scenery of the South Hams, and I welcomed any excuse offered by a showery day to spend my time with new books. To fiction neither I nor my host was addicted; but he had collected probably the finest library on India in England, while for the rest, botany filled many shelves, and I had opportunity for the first time to study Sir Bruce's own classical monographs upon the poison of serpents.

He told me the story of an extraordinary tragedy in Georgian times, and how Grimwood, after these appalling incidents, had long been empty until his father purchased the property, restored it and rendered it habitable again.

"And now," he said, "the hands of death and decay are upon it once more; but whether when I am gone, a new master will labor here and renew the vanished beauty as my father did, is doubtful."

We walked through the woods, visited a little lake, where the waters of a stream were collected at the lowest point of the coomb, and also inspected Sir Bruce's farms, which displayed a much higher average of prosperity than his own dwelling. It was on the occasion of one of these short excursions that Sir Bruce uttered an opinion that interested, though it hardly astonished, me.

We had viewed a field of wheat already going golden-brown to harvest, and my host invited my criticism upon it. "Collins, my tenant, assures me that this is the finest corn within his recollection," he said, "and he has an experience of forty years. What do you think?"

But my profound ignorance prevented me from any comment. "To me it looks much like many other fine fields that I have seen, Sir Bruce," I responded, "but if your expert tenant is so impressed, then doubtless the wheat is something out of the common."

"American grain," he answered. "Perhaps one of Luther Burbank's amazing hybrids. That man hustles Nature in a manner to cause her some uneasiness surely. Collins is a very intelligent farmer. He only laments that he did not come upon this corn sooner. But I console him by the assurance that the variety may not have existed five years ago."

From this subject we turned to agriculture and thence to the industrial position generally. I uttered a platitude, my mind not really upon the subject, and my interest divided between our conversation and the spectacle of pheasants feeding along the edges of a spinney. "No doubt," I said, "little will be accomplished until there are neither rich nor poor. Surely that is the first step to the desired understanding and amelioration. Yet humanity cannot be made to see that step must be taken and that sacrifice made for the good of the greater number."

Then Sir Bruce brought my wandering thoughts back sharply with an energetic protest. "What nonsense is this, my dear fellow?" he asked. "These are the futilities of thinking that have largely landed the world in its present mess, and I have no sympathy with them whatever. Indeed I despise them. Far too much is involved, and the conditions of 'rich' and 'poor' can no more be destroyed than the climatic alterations of heat and cold. The race must be to the strong, and the promised land will not, I heartily hope, be one of allotments and five-roomed cottages only. Heroes will continue to be born, Granger; and herds of men will continue to follow them, honor them and lift them into the command and control of lesser men. But the heroes of our grandchildren will be very different from the heroes of our grandfathers—that I grant, though such men, when they appear, must be adequately rewarded by their grateful fellow creatures. So far I trust humanity to follow the old paths. Science is hard at work, not only in the head, but also in the heart of mankind, and human reason, despite irrational excursions into many false roads under many false lights, may yet return to the true way in time to come. Sometimes, however, I despair, for this cause: that we do not grasp our nettles bravely, but, for cowardice, pretend they have a right to their place in the border. We are frightened to pull them out and cast them into the fire."

Sir Bruce strove for my sake to be cheerful and throw himself into such interests as a visitor to a strange county might be supposed to feel; but I found that, after all, his brother was not mistaken. A spirit of advancing age began to appear, not only in the domain of my host's mind, but in the matter of his physical activities also. Like many old Indians, he had always been an early riser and fond of exercise; but it seemed here, though the attractive surroundings of his country home might well have tempted him to do otherwise, he surrendered to lethargy, rose late and frequently retired soon after dinner, upon the plea of passing indisposition and fatigue. He often appeared weary, and as night approached, I observed that he became more melancholy and disposed to dwell on sad rather than cheerful topics.

His staff was very small and his manner of life, though he made some efforts on my behalf, in reality naked of all nice comforts or luxuries. Indeed he seemed indifferent to comfort and had often, in the past, attributed his own rare preservation and physical well-being to a life that courted hardship and avoided ease, both of mind and body.

"I am content to be comfortable when I go to bed," he used to say. "If a man is comfortable eight hours out of every twenty-four—both in his limbs and in his brain—he should be well satisfied. How many never are? This is not a comfortable world, and a hard life devoid of self-indulgence helps me to keep a sense of reality that most old people entirely lose."

A man, his wife, and their widowed daughter constituted Sir Bruce's staff within doors. They were amiable and simple natives; but they proved very jealous for Sir Bruce and when, on one occasion, I asked Timothy Bassett, my friend's factotum, certain questions concerning Grimwood, I noticed that he evaded any direct replies. My inquiry was of the most innocent nature and concerned the fabric of the mansion and certain portions of it I had not yet seen. There were some famous ceilings of Italian workmanship in empty chambers, and a coat of arms dating from the time of the original possessors in Elizabeth's reign; but though Sir Bruce had never shown me these things, they had been mentioned by him with a promise to do so. Having regard for Bassett's evasion, however, I did not return to the subject; but then came an evening when my host himself returned to the matter and, in connection with it, uttered statements so extraordinary and contrary to all human judgment that I lay awake for the greater part of the night afterwards, doubting whether far graver mischief might not be developing in him than General Fordyce imagined.

This particular conversation was also enormously significant for another reason, as I shall immediately indicate.

We had dined and having returned to his sitting room—a small chamber opening from the library—Sir Bruce struck at once into a topic already mentioned between us.

"You have not yet seen the curious coat of arms over the great open fireplace in the banqueting hall," he said.

"But I look forward to doing so," I answered.

"It was painted in heraldic colors on the marble," he continued, "and a fragment of the illumination still remains upon the carving. The coat is three bats, or 'rere-mice' as the heralds call them: three bats, sable, displayed in pale one above the other. During my childhood that spectacle had for me a morbid fascination. It was as though the life work for which I was destined already beckoned me. Now I know much about bats."

"Surely all there is to know, Sir Bruce."

"Far from it—little enough compared with all there is to know. The legendary lore of the bat may have a significance after all, though Science, of course, derides it. These 'monsters' as our forefathers held them to be—things impossible to place in the frank categories of nature—were thought to have been created after the transgression of Adam and doomed never to take their rank among those perfect works of the Creator which appeared before man's Fall. The bat belongs to the 'peccata Nature,'—the errors, or failures of Nature. Of such are your griffon, wivern, dragon, or cockatrice. And to such may be added the succubus, vampire, and were-wolf of the Middle Ages. As to living bats, I have seen them and studied them singly and in myriads. The bat haunts in certain ruined Indian temples, secluded from a later civilization and hidden among the jungles and forests of Nepal and the Sikkim, are amazing, horrible places. There I have observed these creatures attain to a size far larger than any I record, because their capture, or destruction, proved impossible. These greater varieties of the species possess extraordinary perception and a faculty of animal intelligence we only find in our domestic and highly developed mammalia."

My eyes grew round; but this was as nothing to what was to follow. "Is it possible," I asked, "that you can believe in the thing still often called 'the Bat,' but what is now more generally described as 'the Unknown'?"

He did not directly reply, but asked a question in return for mine. "Have you ever seen a sheep-dog trial, Granger? If not, I may tell you that it affords an extraordinary example of what, for a better term, we describe as the reasoning power of animals. The dog is directed from a distance by his master to do certain things. He has to seek out sheep, perhaps a mile away, on the hillside. He is bidden to fetch them and pen them in a small enclosure of hurdles. These duties he performs with no more directions than his master's voice. Thus we see an animal whose instinct is developed into reason, and whose mind comprehends and obeys the will of his master conveyed to him from a distance by sounds."

"I have heard of them, and the marvelous intelligence, apparently akin to reason, displayed by these highly trained sheep dogs," I answered.

Then he replied to my question. "There was a time when I did not believe in 'the Bat.' Now I do believe in it. And for the best of all possible reasons. I have myself seen it."

I started, but Sir Bruce had apparently ceased to concern himself with me. He was looking before him and continued, as though thinking aloud rather than addressing another person.

"I have seen this thing. I have seen it on a moonlight night flying above my own woods and over my own house. It is somewhat larger than has been alleged. There was no mistake: my eyes are keen still for all their use. I am disposed to believe that more than one of these beings may exist; and, once convinced beyond the possibility of doubt, I have set myself to examine the events of the past and, if possible, arrive at some sort of explanation consonant with reality. So far as I can yet see, there is a solitary solution to this ghastly riddle, and that itself is ghastly and may well be said to strain credulity."

I did not speak—indeed I had nothing to say.

Then, after a pause, he turned to me and directly addressed me.

"You will perceive now my purpose in mentioning the sheep-dog trials, Granger?"

But he had quite suspended my modest powers of ratiocination and I confessed that, as yet, no connection was apparent in my mind. Whereupon he regarded me with a strange expression that I had not before seen upon his face. It almost amounted to contempt.

"You may fairly be said to stand for the average man," he answered, "and if you do not see, then it is improbable that the majority will see either. Yet upon what other conceivable basis can any intelligible clue be found? I admit the strangeness, the unlikeness to truth, the outrage to experience and preconceived opinions. I admit also the consequent horror, for any outrage to experience has always an element of horror. This thing confounds opinion and experience at every turn. I say, then, that as the dog will recognize and obey a human master, and perform for him operations that he could not perform for himself, being aided to do so by its adaptability and power of comprehending what man wishes and directs, so here, in this living organism we call 'the Bat,' there exists a mentality—far higher than that of the dog, yet lower than the mentality of man—which can be trained and directed, ordered and taught to obey. I see in this dark, living agent something akin to the fabled Efrits, and Eastern fairies and slaves of the ring, who were able to carry out their masters' orders; I conceive of this creature, viewed rationally and without the terror it usually awakens by its strangeness, as an organism almost in sight of reason, yet none the less separated from modern man by a great gulf. I imagine that it may be, as it were, an abortive effort on Nature's part to develop conscious intelligence along a different line and through a different species than that which produced man. She began and gave up, turning her attention in another direction. Thus we have a being—stranded on the way to something higher—a series broken—not a missing link, but the end of an incompleted chain. The gulf between this creature and ourselves, unknown men have in some measure bridged. They have discovered the monster, trained it and instructed it to obey them; they have learned a means to convey their wishes to it; and, such is its own intelligence, that it has comprehended and is now operating and using its powers under human direction."

Upon this astounding theory he talked for a long time, evidently convinced that he was right. Once he broke off and anticipated an objection as though he had read it in my mind, where, indeed, it was.

"You will say that at Rome this creature was not associated with the deaths of the anarchists, or seen near its victims though they perished under its attack. But what of that? We know what camouflage means in warfare and the significance of imitative coloring in nature. The chameleon reflects his surroundings and so becomes invisible, as do many birds, insects and fishes. Even a huge object may possess this power, and 'the Bat' is probably better seen by night than in broad day."

To use a familiar phrase, I could not believe my own ears, and suspected that I must be asleep and dreaming. But there was no real possibility of mistake and when I ventured other objections, he brushed them aside. Never in my experience had he permitted himself such assurance or declared himself so convinced of his own belief. He grew excited and oblivious of time. Then, as the clock struck one, an inspiration led me to distract him from this appalling theme and I thought upon Ian Noble.

"Let me tell you of our evening with Paul Strossmayer's 'super-chemist,' Sir Bruce," I began, when he gave me an opportunity. "His opinions and researches would have deeply interested you, and he echoed much that I have heard you say. He was a modest, attractive young fellow, and we all greatly regretted that you were not there to hear and give support."

But Sir Bruce had shot his bolt. Moreover it was clear that my skepticism had annoyed him. For I could not accept his theory and would not pretend that I did. He showed little interest in Ian Noble, and even declared that no friend of Strossmayer was likely to attract him. He evidently retained his old aversion and distrust in that quarter and, indeed, ended the evening by speaking harsh words of the Jugo-Slav.

"It may be that he and his secret companions have actually enslaved these unknown creatures," he said. "At any rate I desire to hear nothing of this other slave in human shape—the chemist, Ian Noble."

He then pleaded fatigue, apologized for keeping me so long from my rest and prepared to retire. He thawed a little before leaving me; but he seemed to have drifted far from the man I knew, and I entertained profound fears for his mind. Indeed I determined to write to his brother on the following morning and was actually composing a letter while I lay awake through that sleepless night, when I recollected that General Hugh's direction was unknown to me. Nor did I venture to ask for it. I remembered, however, that his address would be known at his own residence in Chislehurst, and decided to despatch my appeal there.

Upon what trifles may hang momentous events! Looking back, I feel little doubt that, had Sir Bruce been in an easier mood and permitted me to speak of Noble and what he had said and thought, not a few valuable lives might have been saved in the time to come. If I had even persisted and made another attempt to describe the young chemist's aims and aspirations, infinite good must have resulted, had my host only been wont to listen. But the opportunity was forever lost. Little guessing how much might hang upon it, I felt only concerned to keep the old man of science calm, and did not, therefore, during the remainder of my visit touch again on this disputed ground. Yet had I done so; had I made a favor of it and invited—nay implored him, for courtesy and friendship, to let me speak, it is not too much to say that civilization itself had been enormously the gainer and the total measure of human happiness appreciably enriched and enlarged in this our time. The assertion must appear preposterous and exaggerated; but subsequent events proved it impossible to doubt that I write the truth.

The fatal mischief was wrought, and two days later there came news that entirely preoccupied us; for the extraordinary information that then reached Grimwood, through the channels of the newspapers, appeared to support the extravagant opinions of Sir Bruce.

The unknown had struck twice in America, and "the Bat" had been observed by many witnesses.

Chapter IX

I See "the Bat"

An eminent man had been assassinated in America—one upon whom the eyes of the New and Old World alike turned at this moment; and almost simultaneously were destroyed five New York buildings, all dedicated to one purpose: the advancement of human welfare. In a night they were reduced to powder, and though the two events occurred widely separated in space, but a few hours intervened between them.

The preliminary elections for the Presidency of the United States had thrown to the surface of politics various great Americans who were as yet only names to the average Englishmen; but among these appeared Judge Greenleaf P. Stubbs, who, by his stern and unsympathetic attitude to any convention of the League of Nations, had made his name familiar and caused some consternation in the Chancelleries of Europe.

He was a Republican of the more conservative attitude, and the early, eliminating contests revealed so vast a body of opinion in his favor that already the issue to be determined during the following November seemed a matter of time alone. Never had the index to a presidential election appeared more certain, and it was already obvious that the party of Judge Stubbs would obtain handsome majorities in both Houses of Congress. The judge had been the choice of the Republican "bosses" from the first, and Europe doubted not that, if elected, he would run in harness and be true to those behind him. The fact depressed European thought not a little; but never was the practical world faced with a greater certainty. Already the betting stood at eight to one on Judge Stubbs—the greatest longshot on record in the wagering upon the identity of a new President.

He had undoubtedly proved himself a compelling force in politics, and warned by the downfall of his predecessor from public affection, the judge preserved an attitude purely American, and insisted that his country was faced with ample problems and urgent needs for legislation within her own mighty borders. He had, moreover, the art of stimulating friendship and preserving it. No man ever enjoyed more devoted supporters, for he was eminently sane behind his own native genius, and a sense of humor barred the way to any megalomania, or self-assertion foreign to the great American tradition. His nation already saw in Judge Stubbs a second Lincoln and hope ran high.

It is certain that Europe did not share this enthusiasm, though such was the quality of this great man that few actually imagined him opposed to the ideals of the League; but whatever the regrets of the Old World, few just persons but felt the shock of the future President's sudden assassination. Indignation swept in a torrent over the United States and was shared throughout civilization.

The judge had gone, for a period of rest and holiday, to the neighborhood of Yellowstone Park, in his own state of Wyoming. There he was staying at a private hotel with his wife and family, and there, at sunset of a day near the end of August, he had met his sudden and horrible death. The details monotonously echoed former events of a like tragic nature; but an extraordinary circumstance centered in the united testimony of the judge's daughter and three other independent observers. All had seen "the Bat" almost immediately after the death of Judge Stubbs.

The victim, walking in the neighborhood of the Grand Canyon of the Yellowstone was alone at the moment of his end. But not a hundred yards behind him followed his daughter, Audrey, and a girl friend. Behind them two others attended the party—a young politician affianced to Miss Audrey Stubbs, and the husband of the friend with whom she was now walking behind her father. All four heard the stricken man's loud cry for help, and all hastened to reach Judge Stubbs as quickly as they might. The two men caught and passed the women, then turning a rocky corner of the way. They found the victim face downward on the earth beside a little lake. The judge's daughter and her companion were swiftly beside them, and while all were occupied with the dead, there ascended into the light of clear sunset a huge object on black wings. It leapt upward suddenly from a patch of heavy reed only thirty yards outside the path; and the four who saw it agreed that the flight of the creature was flickering and zigzag after the manner of the bat kind, but inconceivably speedy. It ascended until little more than a somber dot on the sky, then appeared to drift away up the canyon and vanish into the fading splendors of sunset.

Subsequent investigation for the first time revealed marks of the creature. A vulpine stench was recorded by all four beholders: it seemed an essence almost palpable in the fresh air of evening; but more was discovered, for in the neighboring reed bed appeared a lair, where some heavy thing had evidently reposed and crushed down the water growths upon the mire. It was such a mark as a bullock leaves in a fern patch, where it has reclined and slept; and, what was still more interesting, four deep imprints, two and two, were discovered in the marshy bottom where the thing had hidden. Close study was devoted to these impressions and a dozen famous zoologists journeyed to Yellowstone Park. They discovered the spore of huge, birdlike feet, each of which had three claws in front and a spur behind. Every indentation of the triple claw was two feet long, and from the second pair of impressions, which were deeply stamped into the earth, the being had sprung aloft, for no further sign of him rewarded search. Neither did the lair reveal a feather or hair, though every crushed reed in the spot was examined with scientific thoroughness.

Those who saw the monster's flight described a creature with the wing-spread of a condor but of bat shape. The accuracy of this observation, however, it was impossible to prove.

The dead man revealed the familiar stigmata of destruction. He had been punctured in his left breast and it was supposed that he must have perished the moment after his cry for help was heard.

And almost as soon as the news of this tragedy had sped to the ends of the earth, another atrocious event convulsed New York with fear and anger. About two hours after midnight, one after another, in some cases at a distance of three miles, five great temples of the Christian Scientists fell to the ground. In each case no harm was done to the surrounding property; but a terrific and exquisitely adjusted energy reduced the ornate and massive buildings to dust. Not a life had been lost, though many of the night police narrowly escaped entombment.

Thus to America, which had not unreasonably displayed a large skepticism on the subject of "the Bat," was brought first-hand evidence of its reality in a direct and appalling fashion. No longer could the United States reserve judgment, for they were now themselves face to face with the unknown and the strange, too human prejudices that it revealed. Until this time no place of worship had been assaulted, indeed no building built by man's hands and hallowed for its antiquity or religious significance; but now a creed sprung from new Christian interpretations had been viciously attacked at the headquarters of the movement—an event that gave rise to deep and natural indignation and much searching of heart, not only in America, North and South, but at those centers of activity where Christian Science was gaining ground in England and upon the Continent.

The extent of the movement was displayed by the volume of protest awakened at these intolerant manifestations of power. The world, it seemed, uttered a shout of anger, and the subject, again thrust to the forefront of human affairs, absorbed the attention of all civilized countries. Public men spoke to large audiences, while publicists devoted daily and weekly columns of analysis to the things done and examination of the motives behind them. Some writers professed to see a logical sequence of ideas and a sustained policy inspired by steadfast and consistent opinions. They exhausted their ingenuity in showing how all these events were but the outcome of a rooted, reactionary attitude, and in what manner the unknown's intellect actually operated. They held it to be of very modest dimensions and in every respect "behind the times." Such writers went further, prophesied the future and presumed to foretell the operations to be anticipated from the unknown. Again the wit of man was concentrated on the initial problem of what this creature might in reality be and a thousand suggestions, both idiotic and reasonable, saw print. Among these I was interested to observe, in a letter to *The Morning Post*, the identical theory that had so staggered me upon the lips of Sir Bruce a night or two before the outrages reported from America. The communication was signed "Veritas," and I could not directly associate it with my host, though I suspected by certain implicit evidence that it came from his pen.

Eminent writers for the press augmented this wave of prognostication, and openly warned certain famous and advanced thinkers to be upon their guard and give their unsleeping enemy no opportunity to destroy them. Such journalists outlined the possible direction of coming attack and urged that the future movements and engagements of public men should be kept secret as far as it was possible to do so. Thus Fear crept into the community—the familiar, prehistoric dread of the Unknown—and a vague admonition of panic terror began to be felt, like a black thread running through the fabric of human affairs.

But other publicists and thinkers scoffed at these arguments, and a contrary theory, that won wide acceptance from its initiation in the pages of *The New York Times*, began to be accepted in many superstitious quarters. The man who formulated this opinion declared that earth was, more or less, at the mercy of an evil but potent spirit, and the ranks of spiritualism, now furnishing a formidable body of belief, agreed with him and loudly voiced their concurrence. *The New York Times* pointed to those senseless manifestations familiar at séances of the Spiritualists, and suggested that, as these idle demonstrations were believed to be the work of beings on a low plane of the life beyond death—beings who often intruded among followers of the cult and, by horseplay and crazy antics, shocked the serious people assembled to get into touch with their dead—so now the world at large was faced with powerful but minor spirits, permitted thus to reenter the sphere of their ancient earth-life in a carnal though unfamiliar form. As some from their unseen environment played pranks, rang bells, lifted furniture, sounded musical instruments and even tweaked living noses, so, it was argued, others, greater and far mightier, were now being allowed to return from the underworld and display this terrible power—for divine reasons as yet uncomprehended. Many, however, declared that the reason was apparent enough, and that only through recourse to worldwide prayer and a universal acceptance of another life, which these events were destined to prove for all mankind, would relief come. It was, in fact, widely declared that the demonstrations were supernatural, and that by the means of supernatural religion alone, might the world hope for any way of escape from them.

The Spiritualists and many from the Churches also agreed with this opinion; but men of science for the most part declined to entertain any idea so irrational. They believed that human research had discovered the secret of the coming energy; but that those who held the power declined to make it public, preferring to exploit it, that their own narrow and fruitless opinions might be imposed upon all. They also pointed out, correctly enough, that the operations of the unknown by no means shocked humanity as a whole. The results achieved were greeted with unconcealed satisfaction by thousands, whose personal likes and dislikes chimed with them; but at the same time, the majority was dismayed, and it may fairly be said that the mystery shrouding these murders created even a larger element of tribulation than the events themselves. This helplessness before the unknown force began slowly to paralyze rational thought and drive great masses to supplication of a Divine Controller; and while Science and Law strove without fear to solve the riddle, nations as a whole tended steadily to take superstitious views and attribute the terror to forces beyond human control.

Sir Bruce I found to be established in the same strange opinions to which I had listened. He held that the most recent incidents supported him; and while, to my mind, as unreasonable as any of those who now confessed a belief in the supernatural, he argued logically from his own standpoint.

"Men's hearts may quail," he said to me as we discussed the matter on a night previous to my return home; "but their heads should remain cool. We are faced with unfamiliar beings employed in the exploitation of an unfamiliar power. We cannot define the worlds of conscious and unconscious, or say where instinct ends and reason begins. These things may belong to the borderland between. I say 'these things,' because the more I hear, the more am I convinced that two at least of these winged bloodhounds are at work for man and employing the new energy under his direction, aided by their own highly developed, reasoning power. For, in these cases from America, the distance between Yellowstone Park and New York could not have been traversed by any known flying animal, or bird, in the time that elapsed between the death of Judge Stubbs and the destruction of the Christian Science Churches."

"A creature of sufficient size and power might perhaps have achieved it," I suggested, and the remark led him into an interesting statement bearing indirectly upon the subject.

"Size is nothing," he answered, "but there are limits to the size of terrestrial life, and the power of locomotion, whether on land, or in air, is determined also. Much unscientific nonsense is talked about 'size,' and few people seem to remember that there still exist vaster mammals on this planet than any recorded by the fossils of the huge, extinct saurians. Sir Ray Lankester has written with his usual illumination on the subject and shown that the existing African elephant is actually larger than the mastodon and mammoth of the past; and though an elephant is a smaller creature than the giant reptiles of old—the Diplodocus, the Atlantosaurus or the largest of all, the enormous Gigantosaurus, whose arm bone measured seven feet to the fifteen inches of a man's—yet consider our still living monsters. Gigantosaurus probably reached the limit of a land creature—perhaps he weighed twenty tons. But Sir Ray, in his supremely lucid exposition, shows how such a creature is small to the largest living whales—those beings whose immense bulk is supported by the sea. *Balamoptera sibbaldii*—a rorqual, known as the 'blue whale'—is probably the largest and heaviest animal that has ever lived on this planet. When the great skeleton of an extinct monster was found in Alabama eighty years ago, the native folk who found it supposed they stood before the bones of one of the fallen angels! Some of these fragments were sent to Owen in this country and he discovered that they belonged to a whale. The ancient naturalists—Pliny and others—wrote nonsense about whales and much later men were no wiser. In 1825, Lacepede talked of a right whale as one hundred and ten yards long! But it is enough to declare that there are living whales that exceed any known fossil in size. A great whalebone whale weighs two hundred tons, my dear Granger, and he can attain this enormous bulk by virtue of the medium in which he dwells. It is the difference between a land vehicle and a ship. But probably two hundred tons is about the limit for a creature of flesh and blood and bone. The materials are hardly strong enough to compose and sustain anything larger."

"And what of air animals?" I asked.

"Flying things must of necessity be smaller than swimming creatures. Air cannot be trusted to carry anything as large as an elephant. This brute we call 'the Bat' was thought to be as large as an ox; and while it would be physically possible to admit far larger bats or birds than we know, yet the limit must be quickly reached for animals driven through air by their own physical strength. I imagine the unknown creatures with which we are faced must be in reality considerably smaller than they are thought to be. The impress of 'the Bat's' feet, as reported from America, support this opinion. They are not as large as we might have expected and, incidentally, they prove the being in no sense a true bat, since bats have not got feet."

"It may not in reality be of the bat species?"

"It may not, or it may be a development of the known animal. It may, of course, be an insect enormously developed. We have no certain proof yet of the natural order to which it belongs. The American scientists suspect a bird. The footmarks certainly suggest a bird, though the descriptions of the wings, 'like huge umbrellas,' point to a mammal akin to the bat. But I do not yet discard the possibility of an enormous insect. The wound that it inflicts suggests a sting, or stab. It may, so far as the death it inflicts is concerned, employ natural weapons. And, to support the theory of an insect, we must remember that far the most numerous species of living things are all six-legged. If one order of creation may attain to size beyond human experience, so may another; if one order may develop intelligence to the verge of intellect, so may another. There are half a million recognized species of six-legged creatures, or insects, against about ten thousand only of the mammalia and fourteen thousand species of birds. Thus we find quite a fair argument, that this hyperbolic being might spring from the insect race."

"A super-beetle?" I asked.

"Why not?"

"And do you still believe that it works for itself, or others, Sir Bruce?"

"For others," he answered, "because, no matter how high its mental power, it could not know what it was doing without human guidance. By direct action it strikes at the fountainheads of danger and cripples those great and threatening movements to which those who control it are opposed. In my own case, frankly, I do not find much to quarrel with, and thousands and thousands of other men of good will, who share my convictions, must view these terrible events with equanimity if not actual satisfaction."

Then he asked me my own opinion.

"What do you feel, Granger? Do you not see that, if persisted in, these manifestations will not only reorganize thought, but also command conduct? The effects are calculable, if the power continues consistent. We perceive what it disapproves; and how is man to develop any policy, or proceed on any new principles of socialistic government, or false religious theory, if those who wield this weapon choose to intervene and stop him?"

"Of course he cannot," I admitted. "The energy that has obliterated these gigantic buildings in New York might as easily be directed upon Westminster Abbey, or the Houses of Parliament. It is so far considerate for human life and only kills those who must be supposed its unconscious enemies; but no doubt it could as easily attack a nation as an institution, an army as an individual."

"Or a navy," said Sir Bruce. "Earth and sea are alike within its dominion; this unknown energy, which disintegrates a man's blood and bone, or masses of solid stone and steel, could doubtless fling our mountains into our oceans, or lift our oceans to overwhelm the solid earth."

"It could certainly sweep all life before it," I admitted, "as a kettle of boiling water destroys a nest of ants. One prays, indeed, that you are right, Sir Bruce, and that human heads and human hearts control this awful power. That is the world's only hope."

"It is true they might strip the face off the earth, as we peel the rind of an orange," he answered; "but when you say you hope the unknown have hearts, I echo your aspiration. Indeed I firmly believe it is so. If I did not, I should share the general dismay and gathering fear—the herd instinct that is bringing vast numbers of the people to kneel in supplication to their Maker, who holds this energy and all energies in the hollow of His hand. I argue from what is done to what may be done, and entertain no apprehension that any diabolic, anti-human turn will be given to affairs."

He talked in this strange strain and exhibited a sort of fitful cheerfulness between his more gloomy predictions. He entirely dismissed the paramount mystery from his conversation and proceeded upon social questions, linking them in most cases with the organizations, or societies, which stood for them in the world. He returned to "the Bat" again before we retired, and was later to bed on this occasion than ever I remembered him. He drank more stimulant than usual and to some extent came out of his shell, giving me a glimpse of a man who seemed younger in his opinions and more generous in his criticisms than the Sir Bruce I knew.

I reflected before I slept and strove in vain to traverse once more the immense extent of the ground that had occupied his thoughts during the time between dinner and his retirement; but I could not gather up half the threads, or retrace a quarter of the arguments. I concentrated upon the subject that had interested me most, and it was then, to the sound of pattering rain upon the casement and at the first light of a gray dawn, there shot into my head a disquieting and almost horrible suspicion. Was it within the bounds of possibility that this little, highly strung man, his back bent by a lifetime of study and his forehead furrowed with mental labors, could know more of the mystery than he pretended—more than anybody knew? Tonight he had spoken with far greater conviction, far less reserve, than was his custom. He had almost suggested one who stood within the councils of the unknown, for he had scoffed at the predictions of the newspaper writers and laughed at their prophecies; he had declared his shame and despair for humanity before the theories of spiritualistic interference; he had alleged that this and that would most certainly happen and suggested the possibility that other extraordinary events might presently occur. My memory was not good, but I recollected a few of these suggestions and determined to set them down next morning for future reference.

And then, really worn out, I found a laugh awaiting me on the edge of sleep and the absurdity of these musings became suddenly apparent. That Sir Bruce, of all people, should be in "the Bat's" secrets suddenly presented itself as a proposition so ridiculous that I laughed aloud. I decided that the little man was possessed, as so many people now admitted themselves to be, by this engrossing and disquieting subject. I explained the situation to myself, and as I did so, my smiles swiftly faded, for if this fear happened to be correct, then my friend might too speedily sink from his old, high plane of intelligence and drift into something akin to monomania. I remembered the effect of the air raids upon peoples' nerves during the war, and guessed, fairly enough, at what far more dangerous influences might be brought to bear on weak humanity, under conditions equally horrible, but worse, by reason of their unexplained nature and purpose.

Sir Bruce had said many astounding things of late, from the moment that he solemnly affirmed "the Bat" had appeared to him above Grimwood. After that assertion he had proceeded to others even more improbable. Was he already a prey to hallucinations that might increase and confound his intellect? I began to be seriously agitated and once more determined to write to his brother on my approaching departure.

I had, until now, rather prided myself upon a certain influence, that in my judgment was responsible for an improvement of Sir Bruce's health and spirits. Twice, indeed, he assured me that this was the case and acknowledged handsomely my anodyne qualities—in reality the commonplace and moderate opinions of an everyday man. But tonight I feared and my satisfaction diminished.

With the morning, however, I found him in splendid spirits and good heart. He spent my last two days at Grimwood much in my company, deliberately banished from our topics of conversation all unpleasant subjects, dropped the present and dwelt rather on the humorous and social life of his past in India. I had never seen him more cheerful or self-possessed, and my fears receded and actually vanished by the night before my departure and return home.

But then a terrible incident came under my own observation, and it is to be feared that the line I took in connection with it was not that of a wise or courageous man.

I am, however, in no concern to intrude any apologies for my character upon this narrative. The matter is far too tremendous to awaken temptation in that respect, and I claim no credit for anything but honesty.

Sir Bruce devoted the last day of my visit to pleasure and took me, in a little Ford motor car, to the town of Salcombe by the sea. The excursion led into many beautiful hamlets and over rivers, through a fertile region rich in promise of harvest and golden with ripening corn. We inspected the charms of the little township, walked over silvery sands uncovered by the tide, sailed out to the harbor mouth for an hour, then returning ashore, climbed to the summit of a lofty hill, and enjoyed a vision of the South Hams undulating for radiant miles northward and only ended by the gray border heights and saliencies of Dartmoor.

After our adventure the master of Grimwood was cheerful and gracious. He dined with good appetite and sat chatting until about eleven o'clock, when he took his leave of me.

"You will be off before I rise," he said. "The Ford shall be round in ample time to catch your train at Brent. Thank you heartily for your valued companionship, my dear Granger; it has been a source of the highest satisfaction to me, and I hope, now that you are introduced to Devon, you may be tempted to repeat your visit next year."

"You will not be lonely long, I hope, Sir Bruce."

"No. My brother returns for our modest shooting about mid-September; and he will certainly find me in better health and spirits than when he left me."

My host shook hands heartily, looked forward to our next meeting, when he should return to Chislehurst for the winter, and left me for his own apartments; while I took my cigar and strolled a little while upon the neglected terrace. The night was close and one felt that the brooding cincture of its woods kept the air from Grimwood. But that was the reason for the luxuriant growths and general fertility of forest and all vegetable things within this spacious vale. A summer moon had ascended and hung, as it seemed, moodily above the dense, black regiments of the woods. Cloud drifted up from the south, so tenuous at first that it merely drew a veil over the silver brightness from above; but it seemed that the vapors thickened, and I observed a flicker of summer lightning playing far distant above the confines of the sea. The possibility of a storm attracted me—it would cool the close air; but as yet there was no promise of an immediate change. The moon climbed slowly, pursued by the cloud drift from the south; a heavy silence hung over the earth and the grasslands spread very white to the belt of forest beyond. I felt the grass:

there was no dew—another sign of possible change—and then I strolled to the "haha" that separated Grimwood garden from the meadows, descended by half a dozen steps and walked towards the woods. I was in a mind to revisit a little glen, distant half a mile from the house and sequestered within the radius of the trees. It was an exquisite spot—a lake of primroses in spring, so Sir Bruce had told me, and afterwards clad and scented with bluebells. I had only seen it in its high summer splendor of the brake and birches, whose shining stems sprang round about the dingle, where it spread at this season waist-deep in the fern. Hither I had sometimes brought a book and drowsed through a hot afternoon with only rabbits, or a screaming jay for company.

The clouds still lumbered overhead and at wood edge I heard the gentle sigh of wind. The moonlight, obscured from time to time, broke out again and splashed the woodland way with white light between ebony shadows. I crossed the empty hayfield and plunged into the trees by a gamekeeper's path that led to my destination. Only an owl shouted, and from the distance, his hollow voice dwindled to a murmur, another answered him. A dozen glimmering scuts flickered and vanished as I reached the glade, and I stood for a moment beside a great birch and admired night upon that still and beautiful spot.

Suddenly the light was darkened, but by no cloud. A black shadow fell and moved upon the moonlit fern, and looking upward I perceived an enormous winged object flying above the treetops. For a moment it had crossed the disk of the moon and so attracted my eyes. It appeared to be a gigantic bat that wheeled once, then hovered directly over the glade, so steadily that the light from above ran a streak of silver along its inkblack pinions. Now it slowly descended into the dell, not fifty yards from me. I stood beside the birch, saw the monster alight, like a bird with its wings lifted above its head, and then furl them to its sides, bird-fashion. But as it did so, I sank into the fern and crept behind the stem of a tree, lying for some moments silent and in extreme terror. My fear was that the creature might have observed me and had descended for that reason.

Somebody it had indeed observed, as the future proved, but not myself.

For a considerable time I lay motionless, then, hearing nothing, rose upon my knees and peeped stealthily from behind the birch. Moonlight showed the thing standing where it had settled. I saw its long neck; its low ears set far back upon a snake-shaped head, its large, open eyes of phosphorescent green—the sort of illumination now familiar to me as the light from glowworms. The mass of its body was hidden by the fern and I could only see its head and neck and the hump of its shoulders rising above them. Its head moved and I sank behind my sheltering tree. Then thicker clouds drifted over the moon, and for the space of some minutes everything was dark. I looked again, but could only perceive the light of its eyes fixed and steadfast. Once for a moment they went out, then reappeared. It had shut them and opened them again. It appeared to be larger than any reports of it; but I could not judge, since the lower portions of its body were hidden.

The clouds thinned once more and, even in that absorbed moment, I was conscious of a whisper from the leaves and a sigh overhead which told that rain had begun to fall. And then, when the moonlight was strong enough, I peeped again and my heart stood still. For the creature's head was bent, and beside it stood a man.

I could not recognize him, but perceived the two stood mouth to mouth, and I strained for any murmur of sound, or any sign that might indicate monster and human being were interchanging thoughts. To my frenzied fancy there once came the tones of a human voice; but it was impossible to be assured of this; though a sound not human I certainly heard. It was a low and intermittent gurgle, like a bird's note. This sound reached me and soon ceased, but no distinguishable word answered it. The whole scene must have been in reality very brief, though it stretched, as a nightmare stretches, into an eternity for me, where I watched with my hair bristling and sweat running down my brow. It was, however, quickly hidden by the serious forerunners of heavy cloud. Again the moon was blotted and all plunged into a deeper darkness than before. Only the distant eyes still shone out of it and I felt that rain was descending coldly upon my face. For five more minutes I waited, and then the eyes disappeared and I saw them no more. A last gleam of light broke from above, a fitful flash soon followed by storm; but the illumination sufficed to show the glade empty. "The Bat" was gone and the man had also disappeared.

Waiting a little longer and conscious now of the strange odor reported wherever this thing was seen, I started at length in a drenching rain, thankful for the darkness that concealed my movements. For a moment I stood and frankly shook again before a distant light seen far off through the rainstorm as I emerged from the wood; but this time it was a friendly illumination that hung high over the great porch of Grimwood, where Sir Bruce had his own apartments. There a lamp shone through his lowered blind, and another, under a red shade, greeted me from the French window through which I had emerged half an hour before.

I thankfully regained the house, but with jarring nerves and something very like palpitation of the heart. I then shut and locked the windows, helped myself to a stiff tot of whiskey, extinguished the lamp, lighted a candle and threading the silent passages, reached my own room.

My first thought was to approach Sir Bruce without delay and describe all that I had seen; but honestly I dreaded to do so. I felt scarcely master of myself before the complicated horror of what I had seen, nor could I bear to reflect upon it, or consider its implications. Such a common-sense mind as I possessed might doubtless have been expected to approach the phenomena without any distraction, for I lacked imaginative powers and was not sufficiently inventive to pile horror upon horror, or develop the situation in my thoughts; but the actual event proved more than enough to unsettle me. The stark fact that some unknown creature had come down to earth and conversed with a man afforded sufficient matter to confound me. Nor could I suppose that any other than the master of Grimwood had met this thing by appointment in the night-hidden forest.

I longed for time to pass, that I might see again the light of day, and I doubted not that "the Bat" was even now upon some mission the purpose of which another four and twenty hours would probably reveal. I believed most thoroughly that I had seen Sir Bruce himself, and I sank into haunted sleep under that conviction. But with day there came doubts of such a suspicion, and subsequent events convinced me that this dreadful fear was groundless.

Chapter X

From Russia to China

I returned home to find that my friend Leon Jacobs and Paul Strossmayer were both back; while a week later Jack Smith completed his holiday and Merrivale Medland also reappeared among us, tanned very brown by southern suns. The lawyer's walking tour had apparently done him good, for though he exhibited no cordiality, Smith took occasion to express regrets at a past ebullition of temper, and Leon was quick to meet him halfway.

Certain events in his own country combined to atone for Paul Strossmayer's disappointments in another. For Greater Serbia had determined its future constitution on lines that Strossmayer considered to be dignified, advanced, and wise. Jugo-Slavia was declared a hereditary monarchy with the Karageorgevitch dynasty affirmed upon the throne. Her Ministerial Councils had assembled and taken this important decision. The Councils expressed themselves in favor of a unified State with a single legislative Parliament, supported, however, by a system of nonlegislative, local autonomy throughout the new Empire.

I well recollect our friend's satisfaction before these facts, and how, with almost childish pleasure, he dwelt on every detail, even to the heraldic devices of his country. The royal arms would be a double-headed, white eagle, with the symbols of Croatia and Slovenia upon its breast; while the national ensign was designed in a combination of three colors: blue, white, and red. Strossmayer's disappointments were concerned with America, where his quest for young and aspiring radio-chemists had proved unproductive. Such men as he needed did not lack; but he found their own country valued their services and was quick to offer them such inducements that no temptation existed to seek fame and fortune afield.

"America," he said, "has sane millionaires who foster research. Her public is better educated than yours: you have only got to read her new books on science and philosophy to see it. She has even a misty feeling that pure research is worthwhile, simply as a quest for truth. But she is intensely practical also. She appreciates radioactivity and its tremendous approaching significance. The commercial, industrial and protective possibilities lying before her chemical researchers are clearly seen and grasped by their own countrymen. In the United States the chemist is somebody. His may be the 'big noise,' as they say, tomorrow."

Yet one circumstance, which he did not hesitate to impart, atoned in great measure for Strossmayer's transatlantic failure.

"After all," he confessed, "there is not any among them who, to my knowledge, has yet gone as far as Ian Noble. While I was away, his work has progressed amazingly. He stands a head and shoulders above the best in America, or the Southern Republics, and rapidly gains upon our unknown rivals. Ian is, in truth, far along the road to the goal, and has shown me some staggering things since I returned. But he works too hard. I have ordered him to take some rest and get away from his laboratory for a week or two. It is doubtful, however, whether he will do so. I find in him an element almost of fear that he may be too late, so to speak, and fail to catch the unknown in time. He takes a gloomy view of what has already happened and what may happen at any moment."

This statement deeply interested Jacobs and myself.

"Has Noble developed his theory of the unknown?" inquired Leon, and Strossmayer answered, "Yes." Upon that point, however, he had not very closely examined his protégé.

"Details do not particularly interest me, now that I am convinced these secret agents are sound in their politics and can be trusted," he replied, "but Noble has a new theory which needlessly disquiets him. We are, of course, not agreed on the performances of the unknown, and he does not applaud them so heartily as I do."

"Has he changed his opinion, that 'the Bat' itself is a myth?" asked Jacobs, and the other admitted that he had.

"'The Bat' still puzzles him," he answered, "but that slippery customer may also be within his grasp ere long."

Strossmayer exulted in the assassination of Judge Stubbs. He held republican ideals unworthy of a mighty nation, and recounted the effect of this political murder, as it had come under his own eyes. He informed us that he had been in Chicago at the time, and never remembered to have seen such a display of emotion as the announcement caused.

"The judge was as good as elected," he declared, "and it is idle to say that his death did anything visible to depress his party. It made them stronger and more determined than ever to keep their fingers out of the stew pot of Europe; it drew many doubtful ones to the Republican side, from indignation that secret enemies had chosen this dastardly way of fighting. No: it did not weaken the Republicans; but I nonetheless feel satisfaction, because Judge Stubbs was a very powerful man—a personality—and they will not easily find another so great to fill his shoes. Their theory of government is, to my mind, opposed to any generous international understanding. It was selfish and somewhat self-centered, as Stubbs expounded it, and I hope the new leader may prove more ready to value the spirit of the League of Nations and make it easier for America to enter in, when she finds Europe ready and willing to welcome her wisdom. A vast American majority, as I believe, feels no aversion from the idea, and all, of course, know, as Europe knows, that the League without the United States is Hamlet without the prince—a fatuity. Only an unfortunate accident of presentation has delayed our future accord; and for that, not Europe, but a past President of their own is responsible."

"They will come in at their own time and in their own way," prophesied Jacobs. "And royally welcome they will be."

Strossmayer returned to the unknown energy and spoke strongly.

"We think so much alike—these secret people and Jugo-Slavia," he said, "that we would gladly pay a million of money to get into touch with them. They doubtless need what we could furnish—wisdom—and Noble, who is really most interesting on this subject, believes that our unknown friends are at a loose end, as you say, and lack certain, guiding, philosophical principles without which no great movement can be advanced. It is summed up in that. But how to let them know? How to offer the hand of friendship?"

The question offended some who heard it.

"I would not willingly touch a hand red with the blood of my fellow creatures," declared Bishop Blore. "Your perspective is faulty, Strossmayer; you do not estimate these enormities in their true relation to righteousness, justice and civilization. To do confessed evil, that good may come, has no excuse and admits of no palliation on any ethical grounds."

A week later the Jugo-Slav invited Jacobs and myself to see Ian Noble in his laboratory, and though no date for the visit was fixed at that time, we gladly consented.

"Only you two," he said, "because you comprehend me and are men of honor and to be trusted. The others do not understand. They think I am 'the Bat,' and that, when night comes, I grow wings and claws and set out to rob men of life. You cannot convince an Englishman that he is mistaken. Once an idea has entered into his brain, there is no escape for it. He will never set it free. It becomes fixed, and grows, and thrusts out all else, as a cuckoo thrusts other fledgelings out of his foster-mother's nest. But Jacobs is different. He is not English by blood and retains the breadth and balance of the East. He comprehends that opinions are stagnation, death and decay; that only ideas move and keep sweet. You shall come, and of course you promise that nothing you may see or hear shall be divulged. Indeed I will ask you to keep the visit itself a secret from everybody in the Club of Friends."

The thought of seeing young Noble again gave us both pleasure; for we admired not only the genius, but the humanity of the man. For my part I felt that he was high-minded and single-hearted, and I was sure that if any supreme discovery rewarded his researches, he would not permit it to be employed in a reactionary or antisocial manner. I reminded Paul Strossmayer of the past and the little altercation between him and Noble on this point; but he declared that differences hardly existed between them, and that in no sensible manner did he, or those he represented, suffer in their ideals by comparison with Noble himself.

"We are not soulless materialists in Jugo-Slavia," he asserted on the occasion of a full club-room, when November had come and we were all returned. "No, no; and if anything I have ever said induces that suspicion, as I know too well it has, then rest assured you wrong us. We seek the promise of the new chemistry, because along that line the world's future must lie; but for no selfish purpose do we pursue these objects. We cannot do worse than what the world has already done; we shall, as a matter of fact, do far better."

"Why do you say you cannot do worse than has been done?" asked General Fordyce, who was among those who did not love Strossmayer. But his brother, not the foreigner, replied.

"So far he is right enough. The world has made of Science a slave to war, has it not? She was drawn in by the tentacles of that dreadful devil-fish, as every other human activity and energy; and fools have pointed to the fact and found in it a malign interpretation adverse to Science. Well may the new nations promise to do better than the old! They ought to do better. Did Science make the war? Did Reason, whose high priestess Science is, plunge Germany into her appalling adventure? No, Hugh."

Jack Smith supported Sir Bruce.

"As Art is prostituted, so may Science, or Religion, be," he said. "You can no more blame the chemists for helping to win the war, since we had to win, or perish, than you can blame the painters who drew recruiting posters, or the poets who fired the nation's heart with hope and trust in the righteousness of victory. All means had to be pressed in. It was not the fault of Science that she was summoned to assist in an issue of life and death."

I remember that conversation somewhat vividly, for on the following day there came the announcement of half a hundred murders, and there fell one who had towered more vastly in the imagination of men than any since Napoleon. The Dictator of Soviet Russia perished on the occasion of a great torchlight procession in Moscow, to celebrate Bolshevist victories in the Crimea; while half an hour earlier on the same night, at a distance of a thousand miles, fell Baron Ozama, a Japanese, long a thorn in the hand of China and the powerful leader of a growing party. He perished from the stroke of the unknown at Wei-hai-wei on the Shantung Promontory.

In the latter case, which occurred at nightfall in the garden of the Japanese Legation, "the Bat" had again been seen and fired upon at close range as it ascended from behind a thicket near the fallen statesman. The baron cried out loudly when struck, and a guard at the entrance of the gardens was in time to see the destroyer rise. But his bullet had made no impression, if indeed the creature received it, for, darting upwards, it instantly vanished.

In the case of the great German Jew, whose theory of human progress was already exploded, the attack had been deliberately made from the air, and his destruction threw some light upon "the Bat." But it was of a nature to increase man's fear. The creature had rained death and evidently been concerned to make no mistake.

Not only the obvious object of its attention, but half a hundred men who surrounded the Dictator and protected him against any assassin's bullet, knife or bomb, were slain with him.

He had moved isolated in the great procession, with a guard of Red troops about his person on every side, and a space around them, into which no spectator was permitted to enter. But death fell from the unguarded sky; the traitor to humanity fell riddled by a dozen wounds, and with him not less than twelve of his companions and forty of the armed guard that marched beside them. None was wounded only, for a touch of the energy meant immediate death.

For once the world welcomed this new demonstration of power, and many wondered why Russia had not sooner been freed of her supreme enemy. The destruction of this monstrous portent was greeted with the thanksgivings of civilization, and went far to restore a feeling of confidence in all bodies of public opinion not vitiated by the new doctrine. But for those who were more concerned with the secret of "the Bat" than its achievements, fresh interest was thrown upon that theme and new theories of its operations elaborated.

These things had occurred a week or ten days before we visited Ian Noble in his workshop, and I recollect that when discussing them on an evening at the club, Bishop Blore particularly interested me by advancing an argument already familiar from other lips.

"There are most certainly two of these flying avengers, if not more," he said, echoing an opinion that had startled me when I first heard it from Sir Bruce at Grimwood. "I have suspected it for a long time and this proves the fact. The same thing happened in America, where examination of the distances traveled and comparative times will show that one agency could not embrace operations so widely separated."

"If there are two 'Bats,' there may be ten," argued General Fordyce, who, with the rest of us, was now back at Chislehurst for the winter.

But Strossmayer doubted and, once again, showed an understanding of the situation that made many of his hearers the stronger in their suspicion of him.

"It may be as you say, General," he admitted, "yet I see no great force in the theory you advance. The new energy is very likely to be possessed of powers that practically annihilate both space and time. These, remember, are only concepts, not realities. My friend, Ian Noble, of course, follows every move with the closest interest, and the theory of two 'Bats' is not new.

"He has considered it and discarded it. He believes there need be no more than one, because these varied and widely separated attacks in no case actually synchronize. There has always been a respectable interval of time between them—three hours elapsed in America, after the death of Judge Greenleaf Stubbs, before the destruction of the Christian Science Churches; and half an hour separated the death of Baron Ozama in China from that of the Russian Dictator. From Wei-hai-wei to Moscow is, roughly, a thousand miles; but Noble sees no reason whatever why the unknown's energy, adequately harnessed and employed for transit, should not go a thousand miles in half an hour, or, for that matter, a thousand miles in half a minute. He is rather interesting on this subject and points to the freedom from atmospheric friction in the lofty regions where 'the Bat,' if setting out on a long journey, would prefer to travel."

New possibilities were thus opened and a new theory of the thing men agreed to call "the Bat." It was clear in what direction Noble's opinion inclined him—an opinion directly opposed to that of Sir Bruce and to my own, since I had seen what I had seen.

Indeed Jacobs now concentrated upon the point. "If your friend is right," he said, "the theory of a conscious and living creature comes to grief and is left without support. For I suppose nobody—scientific or otherwise—is going to pretend that a living organism could travel through the air on its own impulsion at a thousand miles in thirty minutes."

"No," answered Strossmayer. "If there be only one, then 'the Bat,' as a bat, or anything with life in it, is done for. Life it may indeed contain, but human life."

"Exactly!" cried our Spiritualist, Medland. "Haven't I always said a human life has chosen to conceal itself in this horrid shape—a disembodied being?"

"You always have," confessed Strossmayer; "but, as a sane man, I have always protested against that notion. The human life which I speak of as controlling 'the Bat' is still in a human body, Mr. Medland. In other words Ian Noble has come to the conclusion that 'the Bat' is a machine, and that it is not only employed to liberate the new energy as its masters direct, but is itself driven and controlled by the same tremendous forces. He argues from this that our secret and successful rivals have a very wide understanding of their discovery, and the nearer he himself approaches to the discovery, the more impressed he becomes with the genius of those who not only found out the energy, but also developed a means to exploit it at will and with exquisite control."

I ventured to concentrate my attention upon Sir Bruce during this interesting conversation and, unobserved, took the most careful note of his attitude while Paul Strossmayer spoke. For it seemed to me that these opinions must strike directly at his own. If Noble were on the right track, then Sir Bruce must be absolutely mistaken. And yet my personal knowledge and experience led me to believe him on sounder ground than the radio-chemist. For had I not seen "the Bat" with my own eyes and observed a thing which gave a hundred evidences of life? And had I not actually seen a living man in communion with the creature? It is true the experience had lost its clear-cut outline now that months were passed; but, though I rebelled against my own recollection and would gladly have convinced myself the incident belonged to dreams and not reality, that I could not do. The very accident that led Strossmayer to relate the opinions of Noble, revived the past incident with great wealth of detail. I remembered that night of moonlight and storm, and I waited with very keen interest to hear if Sir Bruce would repeat any of the things he had told me at

Grimwood and take up the cudgels against Strossmayer. But his present attitude made the past in a sense more unreal than ever; for it seemed that, even if Sir Bruce recollected the remarkable statement made to me, he was not now disposed to return to his old standpoint. He certainly made no effort to support Bishop Blore's theory of two "Bats," or deny his brother's suggestion of ten; but neither did he oppose the Jugo-Slav, who came armed with the latest opinion of Science.

Sir Bruce sat in his usual place—an armchair near the hearth—and his position was such that I could not watch his face, or mark whether he resented Noble's view. Indeed, when he did speak, he appeared by no means obstinate against it. He had obviously retreated from his old position and declared himself now as an agnostic with judgment completely suspended. Nor did he manifest his former interest. Upon that particular night it appeared that the whole subject rather wearied him.

Invited to pass an opinion on the rival theories of Strossmayer and Bishop Blore, he spoke in his usual voice, with neither the conviction nor interest that marked our conversations at Grimwood. But he remembered them and reminded me of them.

"Granger will tell you that I anticipated your guess of more 'Bats' than one, Bishop. When he was with me in the country, I developed an argument along that line and rather surprised him by an opinion that, after all, we might be dealing with a living organism possessed of high intelligence and possibly trained by men to its peculiar task, as we train the cheetah in India to hunt and bring down the deer. But I have since found the notion impracticable, and I think my brother may be said to have given it a deathblow when he talks of ten 'Bats.' One is awful and mysterious; ten become a joke. Mr. Strossmayer's friend probably presents us with a view more in keeping with the twentieth century. He is doubtless a materialist, hungry to bend the ways of the world to his own measure. We may at least hope those who wield the secret, whatever their apparatus, possess a keener vision than Mr. Noble."

Thus, unjustly and out of ignorance, he spoke, and when Jacobs strove to assure him that the Scot was by no means a materialist, but proclaimed a view of humanity as generous as his own, the older man would not listen. From indifference he awoke to some bitterness, and when Strossmayer, who was incensed at his attitude, left the room, Sir Bruce explained his emotions—an explanation which only added to the unreasonable attitude he now thought proper to adopt.

"I speak as I feel," he said, when the foreigner was gone. "My mistrust of Paul Strossmayer has not abated one iota, and I am convinced that were he, or any of the younger men he mentions who work for him, to come into possession of the secret they seek, it would be a bad day's work for Europe. Strossmayer, under his urbanity and polite mannerisms, is a savage. He does not deceive me, for I am too familiar with the operations of the Oriental mind. I trust neither him nor his subordinates."

Many agreed with the speaker to my regret. Indeed one or two egged him on to define his doubts, and asked whether Strossmayer's confident interpretation did not argue a far closer knowledge of the truth than he pretended.

Thus far, however, Sir Bruce would not go, and he gave his reason.

"He knows nothing," he said. "Of that I am assured; for if he did—if his friends had found the power and the means to employ it, be very sure that Jugo-Slavia would swiftly occupy a potent and sinister position in the commonwealth of nations. As yet I do not fear him; but I certainly do not trust him; and I have never trusted him. His opinions are unsound and his words are used as a cloak to conceal his thoughts. He speaks with two tongues, and if he were powerful, I should fear him, but seeing that he is not, I despise him."

General Fordyce and many others applauded this harsh estimate; while, for my part, I felt melancholy and mystified, and Leon Jacobs, who caught my eye, clearly shared my confusion. Indeed I dated subsequent gradual changes in Sir Bruce from that conversation and proved, at least to my own satisfaction, that this intemperate and biased attitude was but a symptom of a wider indisposition, which slowly but surely settled upon his intelligence. He began to grow old, as General Fordyce regretfully declared, before subsequent evidences of an uneven mind; but it was Sir Bruce's mental, not his physical, health which appeared to suffer. Indeed in body he was as energetic and unsparing of himself as usual.

To me, and to all of us individually, he preserved his customary courteous bearing and consideration for intellectual attainments not equal to his own; but in argument he now began to lapse from his old, reasonable attention to the views of those who might differ from him. He suffered opposition less peacefully, often made a personal question of differences in reality only a matter of opinion, and, what was curious, talked far more than he was wont to do and emerged from being our most silent member into one of the most garrulous. In the past he seldom contradicted a speaker, even though he might entertain opposite opinions; now he was prone to do so. His pessimism increased, and other marks of weakness also appeared, for I do not think that the gloomy views he took were the result of any theory of a Supreme Being, whose ways were not as ours, so much as a constitutional attitude of mind, which, by its natural bent, reacted against any hopeful outlook upon man's future. He certainly suffered opposition less willingly and, as a very distant mark of weakness foreign to his former self, displayed an eagerness to be confirmed by other men in what he asserted. I do not, however, wish to convey the impression that Sir Bruce had lost all his former perspicacity and acumen. He was shrewd enough still and, upon his own subjects, as clear and magisterial as ever. He manifested at this time a deep interest in the gravitational theory of Einstein, highly approved of it and endeavored, without much success, to state relativity in terms that should bring the implications of the new knowledge into the domain of philosophy.

He watched the progress of "the Bat," though with diminished attention, and never hesitated to declare himself in agreement with the operations of the unknown energy. For a time, however, these appeared to be in abeyance. Nothing happened to disturb the composure of the world, and the death in Moscow proved the monster of Soviet government no hydra, for with the loss of its head, Bolshevism began swiftly to decline, thus affording an illustration of an opinion Bishop Blore had always entertained and expounded.

He held that while any formula of conduct containing the seeds of truth could not be destroyed, a rule founded on error was destructible; and he showed how the end of the Russian "Anti-Christ" as he called the vanished tyrant, instead of inspiring his creed with new life, was destined to shorten its destructive career.

We developed at this time a very active interest in home politics, as indeed everybody was called to do for very sufficient reasons, and from being an admirer and supporter of the Hon. Erskine Owen, our Prime Minister, Sir Bruce and, I fancy, many others now veered to an opposite opinion. Presently my old friend declared that this great man was ruining the country's future by his placatory attitude before Labor's ravenous demands. The opportunities to abandon this servile system were not taken; the necessary combination for united opposition was not planned, and a middle class, groaning between the upper and nether millstones of Labor and Taxation, began to perceive that, while it congratulated itself upon no revolution, revolution was in reality taking place. But, as Strossmayer said, "The British middle class is a coward and concerned before all things for its own precious skin." Sir Bruce now held Owen a traitor to his class—indeed to all classes save those associated with Labor—and he marveled how the Prime Minister could still hold the devotion and support of his great majority. I think most of us agreed with Sir Bruce upon this subject, and Jack Smith and Medland went farther. Smith frankly wished that it might please the unknown to return to England and terminate the Premier's activities; while Merrivale Medland desired a second victim.

"May the blessed 'Bat' cast an eye on the Chancellor also, while he is about it," said he. "For my part, speaking as a wine merchant, I find him far the more unendurable of the two, and so does France. Excess Profit Duties are sounding the death knell of enterprise throughout the United Kingdom, for who will sow while this obstinate Minister does not permit him to reap? Who will work himself to the bone in order that his grandchildren shall be saved from the privilege of helping to pay for our victory in the Great War?"

"He muzzles the ox that treads the nation's corn," declared General Fordyce, "and puts upon us a cruel burden, that posterity, with its rich promise of progress and happiness, would be proud to share."

"And the Chancellor dreams of Fame's trumpet sounding his praises in the ears of generations unborn," snapped Sir Bruce. "Far from it! Time will merely display him as a very obstinate and pig-headed person, without sufficient vision to correct his personal vanity. I wonder that his colleagues permit him so to misuse his powers."

"He is worse than 'the Bat,' gentlemen," said Paul Strossmayer.

Chapter XI

The Unknown in Our Midst

My visit to the laboratory of Ian Noble became an accomplished fact at last, and the circumstances attending the event, as well as the occasion itself, will always be very vividly remembered by me and my friend, Leon Jacobs.

For we were called to a small hamlet on the river Thames, not far distant from Taplow, and since the country was now gripped by a universal railway strike, the expedition had to be made by motor car. Deep in the rut of this disaster lay England now, and though a scheme for the employment of voluntary labor was working efficiently, so the newspapers declared, attempts to travel speedily convinced the passenger that this was not the case. The best was being done within the powers of an army of enthusiastic amateurs; but something akin to stagnation marked trade traffic, and the true story stared starkly from all the great central depots and at the docks of every port in England.

Paul Strossmayer met Jacobs and myself at the Marble Arch in a motor car, which belonged to his Embassy. We therefore journeyed with speed and comfort to our destination—a raw, yellow brick building nestling not far from the Thames and partially concealed by a little plantation of growing larches, now naked. Here labored Ian Noble, and dwelt in lodgings half a mile distant from the theater of his work. He employed no assistants at this critical stage of his researches and we found him alone.

He offered a friendly greeting and declared himself very glad to see us; but we noticed a change in him. He was obviously a brain-weary man and his assiduous toil had rendered him worn and rather haggard.

Jacobs marked his appearance and expostulated.

"You're overdoing it, Mr. Noble. You are indeed," he said. "I can see at a glance that you burn the candle at both ends. You're looking ten years older than when we met in the summer."

"And feeling so," admitted the chemist. "But one forgets time and toil on this trail. The hunt is too thrilling, the game too tremendous. I go to Jugo-Slavia after Christmas and can now venture to say that I shall take with me something very much more important than myself."

"You men undervalue your own significance," I declared; and he laughed, for I reminded him of a book which he had recently read.

"We must stop in our place," he answered, "and the average Englishman is very willing to keep us there. His scornful attitude does not change. A night or two ago I came across Dr. Johnson's opinion of men who devote their lives to scientific research, and I hardly knew whether to laugh or cry."

"Dr. Johnson didn't write much to laugh at," said Jacobs.

"But his point of view—listen. I committed the passage to memory, that I might recall it when I was inclined to fancy myself."

He then quoted from the great lexicographer, who appears to have regarded all men of science as innocent idlers. Thus he speaks of them.

> "Some turn the wheel of electricity; some suspend rings to a loadstone, and find that what they did yesterday they can do again today. Some register the changes of the wind and die fully convinced that the wind is changeable. There are men yet more profound, who have heard that two colorless liquids may produce a color by union, and that two cold bodies will grow hot if they are mingled; they mingle them and produce the effect expected, say it is strange, and mingle them again."

Noble shouted with laughter at this passage of massive irony, but Strossmayer was not amused.

"Surely only an Englishman could have written that drivel," he said.

"Never mind," answered the chemist. "He had not read the Report of the Privy Council for Scientific and Industrial Research which has just reached me."

Noble described with enthusiasm the work upon which he labored, and for a time forgot his own mental and physical weariness; but he bewildered us not a little by talking in the terms of his craft and using words which we had never even heard before. Then, doubtless before our blank faces, he remembered that he had to do with laymen and simplified his exposition for our ears.

"The subject is so new and so difficult, and the processes so delicate and complicated, that they have given rise in a sense to their own language," he told us. "To describe them in popular terms is not easy at all. Energy, you understand, depends upon the mass displayed, the work done. The sea, or a waterfall, or a railway train reveal mechanical work. The energy of invisible molecules, translated into work, is heat energy; the energy of still smaller particles—the electrons—is electric energy. All energy means motion, and all springs from one source: the sun."

"Show us a little of what you are doing, and why you are doing it," suggested Jacobs.

"I will," answered Noble. "And bombard me with questions. Paul has accustomed me to questions. He will have chapter and verse for everything."

"Only fair, as I, in the great name of Jugo-Slavia, pay the piper," said Strossmayer.

"The sinews of war are vital and you are generous," admitted the other. "Until our material comes within practical politics, these things that I am doing lie only in the region of millionaire's experiments. That must be confessed; but what am I doing? I am seeking substitutes for our present great storehouses of power. Dr. Johnson and his friends would say that I want better bread than is made of wheat; and that is what every idealist and searcher for truth should want. I am frankly seeking powers that will turn those grubby giants, coal and oil, into dwarfs by comparison. They, and our chemical explosives, do nearly all the world's work at this moment, and we have discovered and applied the energies of fire and water to some purpose already. But what are their energies? We count them in terms of 'man' power and 'horse' power still; yet compared with what is to come, we might number them in units of 'ant' power and 'mouse' power! Yes, from air, or earth, or both, we have yet to summon a radio energy that shall be to these as the volume of Niagara to a child's squirt."

He showed us retorts and unfamiliar chemical appliances, all small and delicate; and by experiment he indicated extraordinary forces developed from grains of matter that we could only see under strong magnifying power; but, as Jacobs frankly confessed, we did not know enough to appreciate in the least the results that he had attained.

"We are like duffers looking at a professional billiard player," I said. "We are so ignorant of the tremendous difficulties he is conquering, that we cannot realize his extraordinary ability."

Ian Noble was patient with us and helped us to measure something of his performance by the help of words.

"Consider the radio-products," he said, "and the emanations, gases and actual matter that these products give off. This is our field, and it explains how I am dealing in quantities of material almost too small for you to appreciate. Radium, polonium, actinium, and other elements were found in pitchblende, and their discovery went far to complete the Periodic Table of the elements. Remember that these elements themselves have only been recognized by man for about twenty years, and their isolation is of such inconceivable difficulty, their mass so utterly insignificant, that they still lie in the region of transcendental chemistry—to all save those we call by the general term of 'the unknown.'"

"Is the Chemists' Periodic Table now complete?" asked Jacobs.

"No—and that is the whole point," answered Noble. "Between No. 79, which is gold, and No. 92, which is uranium, we have, thanks to radioactivity, filled every intermediate space but two. After No. 83, which is bismuth, we get polonium; No. 86 includes Rutherford's emanations; No. 88 is radium; No. 89, actinium, followed by thorium and barium. This we still find vacant the numbers 85 and 87 only. And I believe, gentlemen, that I have discovered, in No. 85, the secret of the unknown!"

We congratulated him heartily enough, and he explained the significance of his achievement. "When one considers how long it took man to learn the secret of fire and water and employ steam, we may well be patient with you radio-chemists," said Jacobs.

"Here lies a force far more tremendous than any displayed by the other elements—more tremendous than all of them put together," continued Noble; "and what is most important and must, of course, remain my secret for the moment, the raw material from which this element is extracted in no way resembles pitchblende. How generous earth may be of it—for it comes from earth, not air—we have as yet to learn; but this we know: the quantity exceeds by ten thousand to one that of any other radioactive element as yet within our reach, including helium."

"Thus you see how close we are on the tracks of the unknown," said Strossmayer jubilantly.

But the chemist calmed his enthusiasm. "He is still a very long way ahead, however," explained Noble; "for he has not only discovered No. 85 in the Periodic Table, which we, too, have done; but he has accomplished a much greater thing and learned to harness it. There remains a still mightier task—the supreme achievement of all—and that he has not yet learned—and never will."

"Shall you?" asked Leon Jacobs.

"With the help of my fellow men—yes," answered Noble almost reverently. "The chemist and spectroscopist," he continued, "would have regarded my new element as isotopic, or identical, with radium and nothing more; but the radioactivist must have instantly perceived, as I have done, that it is in reality something exceedingly different. I am now occupied with the problem of its power, and in that respect have convinced myself that such power exceeds anything of which we have the remotest experience; but there remain to unravel its duration, its rate of change and various other properties upon which will depend its ultimate value and usefulness. Of course the operations of 'the Bat' helped me there. I do not much fear a breakdown as to the usefulness of my element; but I may yet be disappointed, and, after all is done, I have yet to control the unique energy, break it in and set it to work—first for me—then—"

"For Jugo-Slavia," said Strossmayer.

"Then most emphatically for Jugo-Slavia," answered Noble. "For Jugo-Slavia and, afterwards, for all the nations and kindred of mankind. To wrest from matter something that shall help not only man's body but his soul—that is our ambition, Paul—yours as well as my own. And incidentally we shall reveal Science not as destroyer of old myths and miracles only, but as creator of purer faith and grander ideals—not an executioner of vanished creeds, that have helped man upon his way, but the arch-priest of a loftier revelation, whose altar is lifted in the name of everlasting truth alone. These prodigious energies, now within the reach of man's hand, must find him worthy of them, as I most steadfastly believe him to be. And they must observe no base and unsocial purpose, but be employed for highest uses—sacred uses if you like. Then we shall indeed see Science come into her own, as the recognized leader and dispenser of good for all. She will not persecute; she will ask no man to believe in her until he has verified her credentials; her creed will have no validity beyond that given to it by the evidence. But this I know: she will offer us a greater thing than philosophy has yet attained to, or theology brought within our reach—a formula destined to awake that enthusiasm for humanity which still we lack, and which the wit of man until now has proved powerless to create."

He spoke like a young Prometheus, with the beautiful faith and hope and fire of youth. He displayed before us a mind of distinguished quality but small experience—a mind too prone to judge others by itself and credit mankind with its own pure purpose.

But Strossmayer was before all things practical. He displayed no particular interest before this vision of a world reconciled with itself, and asked a question.

"What about 'the Bat,' Ian? Have you thought any more on that subject?"

"A very great deal, Paul," answered Noble, coming back to reality and losing the radiant aura that for a moment had lightened and warmed his lank features. "Despite some evidence to the contrary, I believe, as I always believed, that we are not dealing for a moment with forces directed against us from outside earth. It would flatter my vanity to do so, for if that were the case, I should be first and not second to make the discovery of the new element. But this I certainly think: we are not up against a nation; we are not up against a secret society, or league. If even a dozen men ran what we call 'the Bat,' we should be faced with very different results from those we find. Indeed if a dozen men, or even half a dozen, had this secret, it would soon be a secret no longer. Federations keep no secrets. Doubt would creep into their councils: they would differ on points of policy—perhaps divide, perhaps fall out. Thus their secret might, through the channel of one or another impatient individual, emerge into the world. And in any case, no community of intelligent minds would work after this fashion, or thus apply their tremendous power. For what results accrue to the world at large? Who is a penny the better? All that has so far been done is to create confusion and anger, and indicate, by the commission of extraordinary crimes, nothing more than that certain human ideals and movements are opposed to those of the unknown."

"Perhaps true in every respect but one," granted Jacobs. "At Moscow it did humanity a service—though even that might be denied by a large body of mistaken men; but for the rest, it has altered nothing, helped no cause, hindered no great movement. You cannot kill an ideal by slaughtering its commanding officers. The protagonists of an ideal at any one moment in time are nothing. Truth laughs at time, since only truth is immortal and can afford to be patient."

Noble agreed with these sentiments.

"It follows," added Strossmayer, "that we, who are not immortal, cannot afford to be patient. Patience is no virtue for us short-lived folk."

"What, then, do you think?" I asked, with a strange sensation, almost akin to fear, that I already knew the young man's answer. It was an emotion of precognition most strange to me, for I am a man without imagination; yet it is certain that, for once in my life, I did anticipate the opinion of a fellow man. What appeared singular, however, was not in reality so, when we remember that I already knew facts that were hidden from the others. For, concerning my painful and horrible experience at Grimwood, I had never spoken, even to Jacobs. The event, reviewed from the standpoint of a fortnight later, had appeared so fantastic that, for more reasons than one, it never passed my lips.

"I think," replied Noble (as I believed he would), "that we have to deal with an individual—a man like ourselves, with very ordinary human prejudices, opinions and predilections. He may be a fiend of mischief with a streak of idiocy mixed in him, for genius is often leavened with evil; or he may be full of good will, without that good sense which alone makes good will of any practical use."

"Genius and good sense are not often seen in double harness," said Jacobs.

"Anyway I would give ten years of my life to meet him, good will, or bad," declared Strossmayer.

"So would I," answered his friend. "I would assuredly sacrifice ten years to corner him and convince him, if I could, that his operations are conducted on a hopelessly wrong principle, that he is wasting and bringing into contempt and hatred the power which he controls so marvelously."

"That, in fact, he is making a hopeless ass of himself," summed up Paul Strossmayer.

I found myself oppressed by my own thoughts before these conclusions, yet dared not voice them deliberately, or reveal my own knowledge. Unconsciously, however, I did indicate the possession of some secret information, by asking a question which astonished all who heard it. But to Noble's ear it naturally appeared so irrational, if not childish, that it awoke no suspicion in his mind; neither did Strossmayer nor Jacobs see anything in it save matter for laughter.

"Assuming," I asked, "that what we call 'the Bat' were in reality a living animal, as many intelligent critics still maintain, can you imagine that it might possess sufficient reasoning powers, or even self-consciousness, to come into correspondence with man? Is it possible that this unknown creature, if such it be, could communicate with, receive instruction from, and even obey the direction of, a human being? I imagine an organism with extraordinary physical gifts, and sufficient mind to learn the wishes and follow the orders of a superior organism—just as our dogs, which can do many things we cannot, have enough intelligence to employ their gifts of scent and speed for our convenience."

Ian Noble stared and the others expressed amusement. They lacked the chemist's subtlety, instantly to link up these remarks with the mentality of the man who had made them; but this I could see that Ian Noble did. He looked at me with a new expression—a curious expression combining opposite emotions. He was clearly surprised that such suggestions should come from my matter-of-fact intelligence; but the proposition itself appeared to his scientific mind as utterly untenable.

"You can imagine anything," he admitted, "but one would hardly waste time on such a fantastic theory, while so many more rational and plausible explanations are offered. To imagine a live creature, in the exaggerated shape of a familiar, terrestrial animal seeking either to impart its opinions to mankind or obey his directions and put itself at his service—to imagine such a nightmare might be an easy feat for a professional storyteller, whose imagination is his stock-in-trade, but impossible for me, who only deal with reality."

He chatted to us for another half-hour, explained the spinthariscope and electroscope and showed us other wonderful scientific appliances—some of his own invention; then we took our leave of him; and with renewed advice from Jacobs and myself, to regard his health and give his overtaxed intellect a rest, we left him. But Paul Strossmayer remained for the night, while placing his car at our service.

We never saw either of them again, and ten days later both men were in their graves.

The hideous tragedy actually occurred three days afterwards, and Strossmayer was at the Club of Friends on the evening that followed our visit to Taplow. But Jacobs and I had gone to the theater upon that occasion and did not see him. We heard from those who were present that he had been exceedingly elated and, with a foreign abandon that often marked him in moments of excitement, had declared the future might already be considered as assured to Jugo-Slavia. This he claimed in the light of events connected with Ian Noble. But Jacobs and I perceived very clearly that Strossmayer's prophecies, as reported on this occasion, were not such as Noble would have supported. Indeed more than one thoughtful man in the club that night began to foresee a time when the Jugo-Slav and his protégé must seriously fall out on questions concerning that mighty energy now declared as within Ian Noble's grasp. Indeed, after hearing these things, Jacobs and I went still farther and until subsequent facts showed us mistaken, wondered if the first vague hints of the catastrophe which reached the public might not mean that these men were responsible for the death of one another. I recollect that we were actually arguing the possibility on insufficient information, when the truth reached us. That morning had brought the rumor; but an evening paper, which Bishop Blore carried with him from London after nightfall, made all clear enough.

Paul Strossmayer and Ian Noble had been discovered together dead on a footpath by the Thames, some quarter of a mile from the latter's laboratory, during the early hours of the morning; while the structure which held the young chemist's secrets—a building vividly in the mind's eye of Jacobs and myself—had been stricken to dust by the unknown.

There was a feature of this horrible event which brought back the existence of "the Bat" to men's minds and intensified the vague terror of late somewhat dulled. On the occasion of this double murder, five independent witnesses vouched for the appearance of the creature. The night was clear with a waxing moon, and between the hours of nine and ten, a pair of lovers walking by the river had seen an enormous flying animal circling over the water high above them; a policeman on duty a mile distant also reported it; and a man and his wife, returning home to a cottage not far from Noble's laboratory, had observed it moving low above a wood. The destruction of the laboratory was not discovered until the following morning; but at midnight, some hours after their death, the bodies of Strossmayer and the chemist had been found, where they fell, by a solitary laborer returning to Taplow. He had informed the police, and subsequent investigation proved that both men were slain by the familiar fatal blow struck into their backs.

It seemed clear that the victims were returning to Noble's lodging when death overtook them.

Chapter XII

The Summons to Grimwood

The death of Paul Strossmayer and his accomplished friend created a sensation that challenged the scientific centers of Europe and America. Ian Noble was already recognized as a man of infinite promise. His early career had been brilliant and his genius none denied. His relations with the representative of Jugo-Slavia were commented upon, and it was pointed out to the British Government by those entitled to speak, that any system which ignored the possibilities of such a man stood self condemned. Half in earnest and half in jest, it had been proposed that if Italy could put a veto against her art treasures leaving the land of their creation, so modern states should strictly preserve their scientific assets. For all thinking men understood that the future welfare of every nation must largely depend upon such possessions. But Government moved not and the great Universities, which might have spoken with authority, were ruled by those incapable of lifting their trust beyond the Arts, wherein they supposed the world's salvation to lie.

A fury of inquiry burst out again upon the subject of the unknown, and again the utter powerlessness of man to cope with the adversary appeared. A most disastrous blow against human progress had been struck, and the majority of reflective persons perceived that, in the case of Ian Noble, there had been swept from the world an agent more fruitful of promised good and increased power than any of those who had passed before him. Few possessed much personal knowledge of the dead chemist; but some of these spoke through the Press and painted the picture of a high-minded and honorable servant of Science—a man concerned with the sacred service of truth for its own sake. Their account agreed in every particular with the opinion formed by Leon Jacobs and myself.

Noble's work had, of course, been conducted in solitude and with native caution; but though the principles upon which he proceeded were common knowledge to his peers, the destruction of his laboratory with all that it contained, left no vital material from which his new element might be rediscovered. Indeed, we found presently that Science knew no more than Jacobs and myself had already learned. It was currently rumored that Noble had discovered Element No. 85 of the Periodic Table; but more had not been divulged and few after his death were prepared to admit the truth of the report.

Thus priceless progress in knowledge was arrested at its most critical moment, and Science knew too well that a generation, perhaps more than one, might pass before any future discoverer with the Scotsman's genius would arise to carry on his broken task. But against that, the more sanguine pointed out that the secret was still in the world and, to the unknown, a secret no longer. This insensate act appeared to bring the invisible assassins into a narrower radius of inquiry and tighten the loop around them. Many, indeed, asserted that they must soon be discovered, and that the ceaseless investigation and unsleeping inquiry now awakened throughout civilization would have a speedy reward. A deep and sullen anger leavened man's thought on the subject and I confess to a personal satisfaction that, for once, passion winged my friend Leon's words and led him into the expression of stronger opinion than he often permitted himself. But at the club, during an evening that followed the double funeral, he spoke.

The dead were laid to rest at Taplow and many attended the last rites. Representatives of Jugo-Slavia were present, the Royal Society was also represented, and the Jugo-Slavic family with whom Paul Strossmayer had resided at Chislehurst stood beside his grave. Ian Noble's parents and a young sister came also, while Leon Jacobs and myself followed the small company out of respect for both dead men.

And at the club that night Leon let himself go.

"The malignant brutes may boast the brain of a god, but it is certain they have the heart of a devil," he declared; "for what but accursed jealousy could have prompted the murder of a man already great, a man inspired with nothing but good will to his fellow men? He never dirtied his hands with politics; he never took a bribe; he never sought to advance himself before others. His one purpose was to forward the cause of human knowledge, and his sole ambition, through knowledge, to advance the welfare of us all and make the earth a happier place for pitiful mankind to dwell in. He never thought of using his discoveries for any but the purest purpose, and almost the last words I heard him say were wise and kindly words concerned with this damnable destroyer we call 'the Bat.'

"He was not jealous of it and fully he recognized the amazing skill behind it; but, in common with all just men, he lamented the narrow, bitter, mistaken scope of its actions; and he only regretted that it was impossible for him, or any other large-minded man, to come face to face with this power of darkness and convince the monster of its errors. He longed to explain to those behind the thing that their awful exploits were vain, their ingenious destructions committed to no good purpose whatever.

"Noble pointed out that if a human ideal, or hope, promised real advance along the lines of moral evolution, then to cut off its head was not to kill it. Tyranny, even while triumphant, cannot confound or defeat truth; immortal mind must progress, though man falls again and again upon his journey. He was the sanest, most moderate young philosopher I ever met—a materialist in the highest and best sense—and I say that the power which robbed the world of him is an evil power and the avowed enemy of progress."

Bishop Blore was the first to speak after Jacobs had ceased.

"You tell us that the poor lad wished to be face to face with this thing, that he might convince it of error. But how, my dear Jacobs, could any man convince it, or reach its mentality before he had trained it to understand him, or learned how to understand it? That is, of course, assuming it not to be human."

"He assumed no such thing, Bishop," I replied. "He was of opinion that, within this machinery of terror, there lurked human intellects, or rather a solitary intellect. And surely the argument is unanswerable. He traversed the whole scope of the unknown's operations, and he asked us—Jacobs, Paul Strossmayer, and myself—if it was in the bounds of possibility that a mighty being from another world, whether clothed in the shape of what we call a bat, or in any other physical form, would be likely to trouble itself about our parochial, two-penny half-penny interests—our art, or religion, above all, our politics? And so raised, the question is capable of only one answer. As for the alternative suggestion, he regarded the theory of some terrestrial animal with high intelligence, fetching and carrying at the direction of unknown men, as even more absurd."

"No," continued Jacobs, "these things are human work, and more than that: they are the work of an individual. He must have a mind of enormous genius in one direction—a penetrating and synthetic mind supported by extraordinary natural gifts. As such, if ever discovered, he will take his place among the rarest intellects that have dawned on this planet since Newton; but it is a mind that on the plane of human wisdom and understanding of social life is commonplace, reactionary, peddling."

"It must certainly be a mistaken mind," admitted the bishop. "The unfortunate individual, if you are right, has no doubt consecrated every energy and devoted his whole existence to Science. Thus he has denied himself experience of anything else, and his opinions concerning economics, ethics and social problems generally are worthless. But religion need not of necessity be denied him. A fanatic, however, he must be—if such a man exists."

"Hence these tears," added Jack Smith. "We are to believe that a mental infant is playing with this awful toy. But I do not think so. There is too much method in his madness, Jacobs. He knows very well what he is about and, for one thing, will brook no rival. Probably he never knew the dead men personally, and felt no more dislike for Strossmayer, or the chemist, than we do for the mouse we catch in a trap; but he suspected they were getting too hot on his trail and might presently be a nuisance. So he smudged them out."

We talked on, each uttering his own opinion; but we missed the familiar fire, the conviction and intensity of Paul Strossmayer. There seemed a hiatus again and again in our interchange, when some challenging or provocative remark was uttered. At such moments I waited, from force of habit, for the foreigner's impetuous contradiction, or enthusiastic support, only remembering that he was gone beyond question and answer, when no voice broke the silences. Upon this night both General Fordyce and his brother took their share of the conversation; but I recollect that Sir Bruce was the first to leave the circle, though not before he had enjoyed his customary "nightcap" and contributed his opinions to the common store. He had declared unfeigned regret at Ian Noble's end; but made no pretense of lamenting the death of the Jugo-Slav.

It was not until five o'clock of the following afternoon that Sir Bruce returned to my mind and then, upon the conclusion of my day's work, there came a telegram for me to the Apollo Life Assurance Society, in Cannon Street. Just as I was addressing myself to my final task, a message, very strongly worded, reached me from Sir Bruce Fordyce himself.

"Come to me at all costs instantly. Vital to vast human interests. Take motor. B. Fordyce, Grimwood."

I confess that for fully ten minutes I sat bewildered before this imperious demand. I am a man of no great physical courage and the thought of any unique and possibly painful adventure was exceedingly distasteful to me. The very idea produced sensations the reverse of agreeable and an instinct awoke, which strove to launch me along the line of least resistance. I felt, in fact, a strong impulse to ignore this entreaty. But reason speedily dismissed so cowardly a prompting. After all, I was a strong man. I trusted common sense and told myself that even if it were Sir Bruce whom I had seen conversing with a sentient being from another plane of life—even if that hideous vision were real—then, despite the appalling fact, Sir Bruce would still be himself—a man of honor, of delicate sensibilities and high ideals. But was he sane?

Again I hesitated, yet for a moment only. Sane or stricken, he wanted me, nay, actually needed me; and he spoke of vast human interests. It was impossible to shirk an appeal directed in such terms.

England still lay under the incubus of the great Railway Strike, and though Sir Bruce had evidently got off that morning and returned to his country home, I guessed it might not be possible for me to find a night train for Devonshire. And the event proved that I could not. Inquiry at Paddington revealed no journey by rail possible until the following day; but there was an aerial service to the West of England and airplanes were flying from London by day and night. I had never flown, however, and did not intend to begin. I therefore took a taxicab to a garage familiar to me near Westbourne Grove, and set out to make arrangements.

By chance, upon this very morning, there were indications that Labor and the Government stood on the brink of an arrangement, and before nightfall rumor ran that the railway men had come in sight of victory. Before the event, many tongues anticipated it and declared that the Prime Minister had taken a decisive step along the road already so familiar to the nation. It was thought that he would grant Labor the substance of its demands, while saving the Government's face with certain shadowy and unimportant conditions.

The conclusions which were hoped would emerge from this struggle had not emerged. The fundamental question: "What is wages?" had not been answered. War had played havoc with the old principles of the economist, and the underlying idea of wages, as value given and value received, was a thing of the past. The war had placed every man at the service of the State, and since the State demanded the work, but ignored the old balance between the thing given and the thing received, wages had ceased to bear any relation to work. Labor was in fact receiving monstrously more than it could earn on any rational rate of values. The employer, toiling for a State in straits, paid what his men asked, since their work was more important than the price. Thus the employer got his commission and the State received the goods, paying for them immeasurably more than they were worth save in the false economic light of necessity. The vicious circle had been forged, and "the cost of living" became the excuse for open rebellion against all laws of economy. Labor deliberately raised the cost of living and then demanded the wherewithal to meet the result of its own errors.

It was now hoped, through the channel of the railway strike, that Government would convince the body of workers how, not the cost of living regulates wages, but wages control the cost of living. The lesson seemed half learned, the battle three parts won—then came the bombshell of another defeat for reason, and before I left London, the newsboys were shouting, "End of the Strike!" "Victory for the Railway Men!"

I had little time to consider these things at this moment, however, and my task was to secure a motor car sufficiently powerful to accomplish the journey of two hundred and twenty miles to South Brent at the highest speed possible by night. I calculated to be off by seven o'clock and judged that somewhere between one and two of the following morning I might reach Grimwood, if all went well.

The car proved very difficult to secure, but promise of a big fee presently produced a raking and speedy machine of high engine power and a driver who had been greatly honored for his work during the war. I dined well and bought myself a big fur coat and gloves, for the night was very cold and my vehicle offered little protection against it. We drew out at about half past seven and I purchased a newspaper or two containing particulars of the terms with the railway men. They recorded that the strikers had won all along the line—and, indeed, all along every line. Their large success was obvious, even to those least versed in the details. My soldier chauffeur voiced a part of the irritation already spreading through London.

"Next time," he said, "they'll want the volunteers again no doubt; but next time the volunteers will see the Government damned first. Twenty thousand men have been working like giants for the country during the last three weeks. They won't do that again—not good enough for a Cabinet of Spaniels!"

My splendid car made light of the tremendous journey; but progress proved slower than we had hoped, for the reason that all the great arteries of roadway traffic were congested with every sort of oil-driven vehicle, large and small. A ceaseless stream of motor cars, omnibuses, and lorries rolled steadily out of London, and another stream as dense rolled back. It thinned by the time we had passed Reading, but at no point under condition of night was it possible to put the car to its full speed. We ran, however, at an average of nearly thirty miles an hour and having reached Exeter about two in the morning, proceeded with increased speed over comparatively empty roads, reaching Brent about an hour and ten minutes later.

I recollected the way, and at half past three we turned into the great gates of Grimwood, slipped down through the avenue of elms, sounded our horn, to denote that we had arrived, and soon drew up before the ivy-mantled entrance.

The doors were open; a light shone from within, and Sir Bruce himself, with his man, Timothy Bassett, stood at the portals to welcome me. Bassett took my place in the car and directed the driver to the garage, while Sir Bruce welcomed me in the heartiest possible manner. He had made ample preparations for my meal and walked up and down his study, where it had been served, while I enjoyed it. A big fire blazed and he had mulled a bottle of claret, that I might win warmth from it. He praised my industry and expressed the greatest possible pleasure at seeing me. He was indeed grateful and expressed his thanks with monotonous and needless iteration. But I readily perceived that he was speaking mechanically and thinking of something far removed from me and my supper, while he declared how good it was of me to respond thus swiftly.

He inquired after details of my journey and apparently enjoyed an account of it, but, to my amazement, even when I had finished eating and drinking and drawn to the fire, Sir Bruce gave no indication whatever of his reason for putting this considerable task upon me.

Finding him unprepared to speak, and guessing that he designed to postpone his desires until the next morning, I prepared to go to bed, declaring that he must sit up no longer. Then I noted my newspapers, which reminded me of the incident of the night before.

"The strike is broken," I said. "The railway men go back to work."

At this news he fell upon my evening journals with very keen interest and their contents awoke him into instant excitement. Until now he had been slow of speech and evidently much preoccupied; but it appeared that the particulars which I had brought banished from his mind every other consideration.

He was furious: I had not seen him so angry, so hopeless and disappointed. He permitted himself the utmost indignation and heaped upon the head of the Hon. Erskine Owen a torrent of scornful vituperation and reproach. I stood amazed before such bitter invective, for never had I seen Sir Bruce so swept by strong feeling, or so indifferent to conceal his emotions. "The accursed wretch has filled his cup of iniquity!" he cried. "It runs over, to poison the fountains of honor and weaken the foundations of our liberties. This is a nail—another nail in the coffin of the Constitution. He has abused his trust, defied authority and broken his oaths to his country and his king!"

For a long time he raved thus, and I tried in vain to temper his passion and save the nervous energy he was losing in this futile display. But I argued to no purpose and could make nothing of him.

He talked himself tired, and then came back to himself and his duties as a host. He perceived my weariness and ceased his lamentations. He blamed himself for allowing these incidents to intrude at such an hour, and then conducted me to my room. Only at his leave-taking did he make an indirect, though none the less sinister, allusion to the purpose for which he had summoned me.

"Sleep in peace," he said, "and sleep well, for after tomorrow, your soul may not know peace for many days."

He was now kind and solicitous for my comfort. He mended the fire that burned in my bedroom, asked me if I would take any further refreshment, thanked me once more for my swift response to his summons and then bade me good night and left me.

Thoroughly worn out, I slept as I have seldom slept; and evidently by Sir Bruce's order I was not called next morning but allowed to have my slumbers out. Not until eleven did I awake, and guessed that it had been his wish I should begin the day in possession of all my wits and strength. But no ordeal awaited me, for after breakfasting alone, according to former custom, I waited in vain for Sir Bruce to appear.

Bassett informed me that his master might descend at any moment. But at luncheon my host was still invisible and the gong brought no response. A suggestion that he should be summoned was rejected by his man.

"Against all rules, my dear," he said in his familiar vernacular. "If Sir Bruce be minded to take his meat with you, he'll come down along; and if he ban't, then he'll bide up over. Us be forbade to call him at any time."

Chapter XIII

Face to Face

I felt somewhat alarmed at an event to have been so little expected, and was as much concerned for myself as the master of Grimwood. My time possessed value; and yet it seemed that he had utterly forgotten, both me and the fact that I must now be waiting his pleasure, to the detriment of my own affairs. Such discourtesy was so unlike my friend and delay at this moment so opposed to the urgent quality of the message which had brought me to Devonshire, that I could think of no explanation of an innocent nature.

I approached Timothy Bassett and his wife, to find that neither shared my tribulation. They repeated their assurances that Sir Bruce often absented himself in this fashion and strongly advised me not to challenge him, as I now desired to do.

"He's got his ways," said Timothy, who evidently knew all about his master. "He'll often keep up there for a day and a night together. If we was to break in upon Sir Bruce, there would be a proper tantara, and he'd send me and my wife and daughter going. It would be as much as my place was worth. Once I tried it, so I know."

His confidence restored my own. I determined that I would stop at Grimwood until the following morning and then, if Sir Bruce declined to appear, abandon him. I was somewhat indignant at such lack of consideration; but my anger turned into alarm as the day wore on.

I lunched alone, with Timothy and his wife to entertain me; but though amusing in a bucolic fashion, I could learn but little about their master from them. They would talk of anything and everything save Sir Bruce. Him they exalted into a great personality; but they declined to give any details. The man led me to suspect, however, that he was a little frightened of his employer, and his wife, Nancy Bassett, did not hide the fact that she was also.

"A wonnerful gentleman," she told me. "He knows more'n us common folk, and that's because he lived in India, no doubt, where there's a lot more wisdom than in these parts. He's got an Indian saying for most every thing that happens. He don't like Devonshire people very much. He says they be only your friends so long as you've got a stick in your hand, and that you'll find weevils in a stone afore you'll find sense in the farm laborers about here."

I laughed, and seeing that she amused me, the old woman proceeded. "Sir Bruce says, 'If you've never seen a tiger, look at a cat, and if you've never seen a rascal, look at my husband.' That's his fun, of course, for Timothy's his right hand. And Sir Bruce says that the lawyers and the tailors be too sharp for the Angel of Death and that God alone knows how to catch 'em. He don't like lawyers, nor yet tailors, you see; and he says also that you should change your washerwoman when you change your linen, because a new one always washes clean."

She prattled on, while I ate my luncheon; and still Sir Bruce gave no sign. When the meal was over, I sent for the big car in which I had come, and the driver, weary of doing nothing, proved very glad to take me to Plymouth. The distance was but ten miles, and I determined to pass an hour there, send a telegram or two to London and Chislehurst, read the papers and learn the latest information concerning the end of the strike.

We were quickly at our destination and, turning into a newspaper shop, I was staggered to hear tragic news. England had been startled to its very heart within that hour, for now, the time being about half past three o'clock, telegrams came through announcing that the Hon. Erskine Owen was dead. He had died suddenly one hour earlier, but the manner of his end was not as yet known.

At the office of a local newspaper I shouldered my way into the crowd surrounding the window, and presently won a little further information. The record was scanty, but it seemed that on the Premier's arrival at the House of Commons, he did not alight briskly as usual, and a policeman looking into his private car discovered Owen lying back motionless and apparently insensible. He was found to be dead. He had traveled from Downing Street alone, and the car, as the driver explained, had not been stopped upon the way.

Acute alarm shook me before this dreadful information. Argue as I might it was impossible to help connecting it with other matters in my thoughts. I found myself linking the tragedy with Sir Bruce, and recollected very vividly his storm of anger on the previous evening. Yet I felt some hope, and reason soon supported my conviction that I was allowing false fear to alarm me without cause. Doubtless the truth of the Prime Minister's death would be known before the end of the day. That such a man might succumb to heart failure, under the tempest of abuse which had broken upon him that morning in the newspapers, seemed quite possible to me. For not a journal which I was able to peruse but censured him in unmeasured terms for an action charged with gravest peril to the Nation. Many papers prophesied a future as dismal as Sir Bruce's own prediction. They declared that nothing but the most terrible industrial disaster would follow, and foretold that revolution was practically assured by the terms of Owen's surrender.

Hoping against hope that natural, physical causes would presently account for this sensational end of a great career, I went to a hotel presently for a cup of tea. There was a tape machine in the vestibule of this place and no small crowd assembled around it. Men broke off the trickling message foot by foot, and handed it for others to read after they had done so.

And then it was, while I took refreshment, that there came the dark news that many besides myself had already anticipated. I recollect the laconic wording of the tape.

"OWEN MURDERED BY THE UNKNOWN.
WOUND IN BACK—NO EVIDENCE OF HOW DELIVERED."

Deep emotions mastered me at this statement, and I remember that my first instinct was to return straightway to London in my car and not go back to Grimwood. For a time my excited intelligence associated Sir Bruce directly with the assassination and refused even to weigh the practical impossibility of such a thing. Conviction above logic urged me away from the old man and his country home. I felt positive that he could not be there; and that, even if I desired to see him, he would not be found at Grimwood; but with a calmer mind I argued against this panic determination and resolved to return instantly. For it appeared to me that my own honor must now, more than ever, depend upon so doing. No proof as yet existed to support any suspicions; and even if subsequent events did so, then to keep in touch with Sir Bruce might prove a national duty. If, indeed, he had done this appalling thing, then one could only suppose that he was mad; and a madman with the powers that he appeared to possess might threaten civilization within the next few hours. I was almost crushed under the weight of the possible obligations now thrust upon me, but acted as I believed for the best and, within the space of five minutes, was on my way back to Grimwood. I found myself in a state of nervous excitation altogether beyond my experience, yet strove to keep myself in hand and considered how best I might act if the future put Sir Bruce into my power.

The winter night had closed down and our headlights flashed before us as we left the main road and penetrated the network of lanes to Grimwood. My driver had taken good note of the way and, thanks to a rare sense of locality, made no mistakes. The car swiftly returned, but it was now night and the rolling woods that hemmed in the manor had already sunk into amorphous gloom as we descended the avenue into the cup below. The frost of the previous day had broken and a mild evening was misted by light fog that rose from the earth and filtered tenuously through the tree stems. Into this vapor we threw a great fan of illumination that marked the immediate course of our way, then faded upon surrounding darkness. The mist was heavier below and extended in white layers over the meadow lands—their pallor breaking through the night.

And then, directing my driver to take the car to its place, I strolled to the front of the house and perceived that Sir Bruce's rooms were illuminated. Steady lights shone in the upper storey of Grimwood, and whether indeed he had been absent or not during the morning, he was now certainly returned. I strove to believe that he had never left Grimwood and hoped that he would now descend to welcome me, if he were not already downstairs. I forced myself into a conviction that my apprehensions lacked any solid basis; I even told myself that Sir Bruce would share the world's horror when I broke the news of Owen's death. It was now five o'clock, and remembering that the Prime Minister had perished about half past two, it appeared obvious that my host could have had no direct hand in an event still barely two and a half hours old. Fortified by this thought I entered the house, rang for Bassett and inquired of him whether he had seen Sir Bruce and where his master might be.

"He is in," I said, "his lights are burning."

Timothy seemed surprised.

"Course he's in, master! He haven't been out. Us have got our own electricity, you see, and I'm clever enough to look after it. No doubt, when the dark came down, Sir Bruce lit up."

"You haven't seen him?"

"No, he ain't been about. I reckon he'll come to dinner bimeby; but if he don't, there's no call to be vexed. You mind his ways in the summer. He has his own ideas."

"But he telegraphed especially for me to come to him," I explained. "I motored down last night at great personal trouble on his account, and he assured me that today he would tell me all he wanted me to know."

"Then be sure he will do so," promised the old fellow. "He's a terrible truthful gentleman, Sir Bruce is, and he won't tell you no lies. But he has his own ideas; and all us have got to do be to fall in with 'em, and keep our mouths shut and ax no questions. He's difficult to please sometimes, but who ain't? Life's life, whatever you be called to serve, and us all know that sparks are the lot of the blacksmith's legs."

I considered this. Bassett's saying was evidently a little bit of his master's Indian lore, for an English blacksmith would not expose his legs to sparks, while an Indian one doubtless might do so. Timothy was cautious and secretive as a rule; yet he had admitted that Sir Bruce proved not always easy to satisfy.

"'Life is life,' as you say," I answered. "We must be patient, I suppose. Shall you call Sir Bruce to dinner?"

"Certainly not, sir. I've told you he'll never be disturbed, and he don't allow nobody in his rooms, except in the bedchamber; and only there when he's out of it. He's got his ideas, and if he wants to eat his dinner along with you, he'll come down house and do so when the gong sounds at eight o'clock; and if he don't, he won't. It ain't no business of ours."

"It is my business, however," I replied, "and if Sir Bruce declines to remember my existence this evening, then I shall leave at an early hour tomorrow."

"You'll do just what you think right, I'm sure, my dear," was all he answered.

The uncompromising old chap annoyed me. I felt that he was making a fool of Sir Bruce's guest, though really the suspicion proved unjust. Indeed, in response to my next speech, he became a little more communicative.

"I have a very good mind to go up to your master's rooms and hammer at the door and insist on being attended to," I said; but he earnestly begged me to do no such thing.

"Doan't ee, there's a good man," he begged, with a familiarity that was not in the least impertinent. "Take my advice and carry on as usual. The master knows very well as you be here, and he wouldn't treat you uncivil without a proper reason. He wouldn't treat a house-beetle uncivil for that matter—kindness made alive he is, I do assure you. But if anything could make him mad 'twould be to push in upon him, or break his peace. Only once—four year agone—when he'd been cooped up for three mortal days, did I venture to forget orders and shout and say I must be answered, or I'd fetch the doctor; but I never done it again. He was all right, of course—busy about his ideas—and by gor! the lightning flashed from his eyes when he opened the door and leapt out like a raging lion upon me. Very near sacked me that instant moment; and it weren't until my wife and widowed darter went on their knees to him that I was saved. And so it will be with you; you'll lose the gentleman's friendship for evermore if you thrust in."

As for the friendship of Sir Bruce, it must be confessed that I had ceased to covet that. He was certainly using me ill, and I did resent the fact that he could pursue his own interests, whatever they might at present be, and leave me to cool my heels and wait his pleasure after my great response. As Timothy truly remarked, his master knew I was in the house, summoned thither at his urgent direction, and I could only suppose some irregularity, if not an actual upheaval of mind, kept him in his apartments and left me idle and puzzled beneath. But I had to leave it at that for the moment and, resolving to start for London at daybreak, I went to my room and prepared for dinner.

The gongs rang punctually at the appointed times, one half an hour before dinner, the second at eight o'clock, when the meal was served. I descended at five minutes to the hour, hoping to find Sir Bruce in the study, but he was still invisible. I then strolled to the dining room, where two places were laid on the polished walnut-wood table. Timothy was opening a bottle of claret and had not seen Sir Bruce.

"He'll be stirring at the gong belike," he told me. "You see there's no call to wait upon him up over. He never had his own man and always looked after himself. He's got all he wants in his rooms, and hot water laid on from the kitchen likewise."

At eight o'clock the veteran struck the gong, and as the sound rumbled through the hall and died away along the upper and lower corridors, Ann Ford, his daughter, brought a tureen of soup from the kitchen. Then Timothy turned up an electric light, which hung over the dining-room table, and I went into the hall, that I might greet Sir Bruce on his appearance. But he did not appear. I waited for five minutes and then suggested a second warning, only to find that nothing could induce Timothy to touch the gong again.

"You can go in and eat and drink," he said, "for Sir Bruce ban't coming. He's so punctual as a cow in all his ways, and a thousand times I have seed him turn the corner of thicky stairs afore the sound of the gong was still. If he had meant to take his dinner along with you, he'd have been down on the stroke. Early he may be, late never. He ain't coming, master."

I stood irresolute and exasperated. The old boy carried the soup to the service table and Ann—a quiet woman of forty, who much resembled her mother—prepared to wait upon me. It seemed that there was nothing left either to say or do, and Timothy and his daughter attended quietly till I should take my seat. The situation was absurd, yet I saw nothing amusing in it. Indeed I experienced acute annoyance, while feeling at the same time there could be no sense in displaying any. But the mildest mannered man hates to look a fool through no fault of his own, and I felt not only that these impassive people were laughing at me behind the mask of their pleasant countenances, but also that, despite Bassett's assurances, he must really know more concerning his master's movements than he pretended. The man and woman regarded me quietly and patiently while I strode up and down the dining room, irresolute and perturbed, with my hands in my pockets.

Suddenly a desire took me to gaze again at the exterior of Sir Bruce's apartments and I went to the French window, pulled back the heavy curtains drawn over it and flung it open. Before I walked out, however, the factotum spoke.

"I shouldn't do that, sir, if I was you," he said, and for once I detected a quickening of his slow speech. He evidently had no desire that I should leave the house. Indeed he stepped towards me and turning I saw something very like anxiety and concern upon his face. His daughter made less attempt to hide her feelings. She was staring straight at me and evidently felt alarm.

Much and vainly I have wished since then that I had taken the old man's advice; but I did not. I was nettled, and the suggestion in his voice and action that he would actually prevent me from leaving the house if he could, upset what little temper remained to me.

"Stop where you are," I said, "and mind your own business. I am going to walk on the terrace, and when I want my meal, I'll take it."

So saying I left them and passed into the darkness of the night. I was conscious that both Bassett and his daughter followed me to the window; but they came no further, and when I turned, after a few short strides, they had evidently thought better of it and retreated.

The night was still heavy with an earth-born fog, but the mist was disposed irregularly. It followed the course of the stream, that descended through the meadows, and it dislimned and wound away along the neighboring edges of the woods. About and above the house and gardens there was but little vapor and I could see the stars shining over my head. I padded the terrace half a dozen times and then rapidly grew calm. In a few movements I perceived the futility of this irritation and also discovered that I was a hungry man. I determined to go back, eat my dinner and behave with reason, still hoping that Sir Bruce might be pleased to descend and spend the evening with me afterwards. But, before returning to the house, I recollected the impulse that had driven me from it and the motive: to gaze again at the outside of my host's rooms and observe if they were still illuminated. I stood off from the house, therefore, left the neglected and grass-grown terrace and walked out upon the garden, that I might get a look at the windows above.

The light still burned in them and threw a gentle beam into the haze without. And then, in a moment, I became conscious of some slow and silent movement above my head and saw a patch of darkness blot the stars. It became swiftly larger, and though it was too dark to perceive its outline, this grew fairly distinct in a few seconds and I saw that the object was descending straight upon Grimwood. It became defined in a moment and my eyes, now accustomed to the darkness, made out a gigantic flying animal that wheeled once, then turned and, after remaining stationary with outspread pinions, slowly descended upon the roof of the manor. It settled as gently as an owl upon the battlemented summit, then furled its wings and turned round with its long neck stretched forward over the terrace beneath. The movements were automatic, and just such as any bird would have made when alighting in this position.

The thing had perched immediately above Sir Bruce's windows, and I could see its bat-like head, its ears laid back and the glow-worm light in eyes that seemed out of proportion large to its flat, reptilian skull. They were like saucers of dim fire. I knew at once that the creature was the same that I had observed in the glade during my previous visit, and I waited, transfixed, gasping and staring upwards in the horrible expectation that Sir Bruce would swiftly open his window, or possibly appear upon the roof beside his messenger. But that did not happen and, instead, I found myself faced with an event far more appalling. To see the creature was terrible enough, and I felt my heart beating furiously, so that my breast could hardly contain it; but now a thing far worse befell, for I in my turn was seen.

"The Bat" perceived me standing and staring upon it from below; its head suddenly thrust out; its neck was lowered over the parapet; I felt as though a ray had struck me from its eyes. Even in that moment of terror, I perceived the sudden increase of their light. They glowed and I was conscious of being illuminated by them. Then the thing opened its wings again and slid noiselessly down, straight to where I stood beneath it. As it came the light undoubtedly increased, and I felt myself circled by a ray from which escape into the outer darkness was impossible. As lightly and swiftly as a night hawk it descended, wheeled immediately over me, not twenty feet above my head, and then touching ground some fifteen yards distant, closed its wings and hopped towards me.

I strove to run, but could not move hand or foot. A frenzied instinct to get into the house and so evade it, won no response from my frozen muscles. As in a nightmare I stood, fastened to the earth, all my faculties clear, conscious that a dreadful death must now be the matter of moments only.

Moments indeed they were, but time becomes no more than a word in many a supreme crisis of life, and for me those moments extended into hours—a very lifetime of acute agony. In reality all was over in a few seconds; but they stretched to an eternity.

I struggled to shout my danger and summon aid, but no sound came; then I perceived a man's figure running swiftly from the corner of the house and felt a dreadful regret that he had come too late. At the same moment something seemed to crack in my heart and I found myself falling to the ground, in what my last conscious thought believed was death.

Chapter XIV

Number 87

When consciousness returned I found an arm supporting a glass of spirits at my lips. Instinctively I drank of it and then heard Sir Bruce thank God.

But it was not his arm that held me up. Timothy Bassett knelt beside me and sustained me.

"Have no fear—all is well," said Sir Bruce, and then I perceived that he stood beside me, but in strange attire. He was clad in tight-fitting black from head to heel and his head appeared to be enveloped in a heavy black cowl with earpieces. Indeed only his eyes, nose and mouth were visible. I gazed wildly about me for the monster; but it had vanished, and after a few words, Sir Bruce withdrew.

"Bassett will give you an arm," he said. "Return to the dining room and try to make a good meal. I will join you shortly."

Then he spoke strangely to his old servant.

"Be ready to leave—all of you—in three hours' time, Timothy. Tell your wife and Ann to set about their preparations at once. For tonight you can convey yourselves and your goods to the empty lodge. There you will be safe. And have no fear for the future. All of you are amply provided for."

He left us, having seen me again on my legs, and I now observed that Bassett was in a condition of supreme dejection and misery.

"It's all over; it's all over," he kept mumbling, nor did he appear able to answer the questions I put to him.

He gave me an arm to the house, but I was now recovered and presently contrived to eat and drink. While I did so, Bassett who waited on me alone, seemed concerned for his own future.

"Us was sworn to say nought," he explained, "and I pray God that no evil will fall upon me and my wife and child. We're innocent as unborn babes—the three of us."

Knowing nothing, I said nothing.

Sir Bruce appeared before I had finished and himself partook of a little food, then, somewhat dizzy and unsteady, I followed him to his study. He still wore the singular garments, but had removed his cowl. He was very pale, his eyes flickered with a strange light and the woe of the world appeared to rest upon his forehead.

He bade me take an easy chair and then began his story without preliminaries.

"I shall leave you a brief manuscript," he said, "and I ask you to publish it in *The Times* at an early date. Before we part, I will read it to you. The document covers all the ground of my actions and motives, my ambitions and my failure to achieve them. Together with what I am now going to impart, it embraces the whole story. I have chosen you as the recipient of my confidence, and I know, arduous and painful though the task has been and may yet be, you will not blame me in that matter. That I should have caused you this terrible shock tonight I deeply regret. I had planned not to do so, and only the unexpected accident of your leaving the dinner table and coming out upon the terrace precipitated the misfortune."

He broke off for a moment, then plunged into his extraordinary narrative.

"When radioactivity was discovered and the new elements appeared, I found myself deeply interested in the subject. I devoured the scanty information to be obtained, and fifteen years ago, when on holiday in England, studied in the French laboratories and learned all that could be learned up to that time. A natural bent inspired me, and when I returned to India for my last term of official service, I devoted every moment of my leisure to radioactivity. The story of my labors will perish with the results of them. It suffices that by a strange accident on an expedition in the Sikkim, I found a new element and proved it to be No. 87 of the Periodic Table. The late Ian Noble, as I know now, discovered No. 85, and concerning that I can say nothing. No. 85 has disappeared with Noble himself; but from what I heard Strossmayer say at the club on the night before I killed him, I believed that it was No. 87 Noble had found. That No. 85 possessed the ubiquitous powers of my element I cannot suppose. No. 87 is the King of Elements—whether in this world or any other.

"My element, forever nameless now, and destined to be hidden from this generation with my departure, is distributed under certain natural conditions with the utmost profusion. An extraordinary chance—little likely to happen again—placed it within my reach. I quickly perceived that the supply was enormous and after sustained and tireless experiments, I found myself able to secure the energy at will and in quantity far in excess of any private requirement. For three years I matured my processes and did not leave India until I had discovered, not only the complete attributes of the element—its duration, and so forth—but also the means by which it might be controlled and applied. The stupendous difficulties attendant on radium and other radioactive material are modified in connection with mine. It is an amenable giant.

"What are its attributes, and what its prodigious significance to mankind, you will learn from my manuscript. What I have done with it you already understand, because the facts are common property. I am the 'Unknown.' The events of the last year are my work and mine only. When I left the Civil Service and retired, I came to England armed with my secret; and it was my original purpose to place it at the service of our Government.

For reflection convinced me that to make it public and inform the world of what I had found, might inevitably defeat my own ambitions and desires. But we were now immersed in the Great War, and apprehending only too certainly the purposes to which the energy would be applied, I determined to conceal it. At the crisis, I had decided to enter myself into the arena and win the war for the Allies. This I could have done, and I was actually making my arrangements, when severe indisposition overtook me. For a year, as you will remember, I was a very sick man, and during that year the war was won.

"Again I considered the importance of liberating my discovery, as a healing rather than a destructive force, and again I convinced myself that the danger far exceeded the promise of any salvation I could yet bring. Passions still swept every heart, and well I knew that neither the defeated nor victorious nations might yet be trusted with No. 87. Naturally no thought of self-advancement darkened my deliberations; otherwise, I had certainly proclaimed the find and won the earthly fame that must have resulted to me from such an achievement. But I had long lost any personal ambition in the matter and was only concerned with an agonizing desire to help mankind, and an equally terrible conviction that it was still impossible to do so. The temptation to reveal was fought by the deep conviction that no Government on earth might be trusted with this terrific agent. Again and again I was upon the brink of proclaiming my knowledge; again and again circumstances and the ceaseless revelations of man's faulty ambitions, false ideals, unconquerable savagery and unconquerable greed kept me silent. The terms of the great peace struck me dumb with dismay, and though my secret tortured me, I kept it from mankind—at a cost only I can tell.

"But through slow stages, now seen clearly enough by me, I paid the price of that fearful strain. It wore me down; it deteriorated my intellect; it found the faulty ingredient within my own nature and finally drove me into the actions I deplore too late. I had conquered much; I had withstood the ordinary human weakness for fame, for the applause of my own generation and the honor of generations to come. These allurements passed me by; but I was not proof against myself, and those dangerous constituents of character ingrained in my own personality and now to be liberated by my weakening intelligence."

He broke off for a moment upon a subsidiary theme.

"I am a pessimist," he continued, "and we will consider that for a moment. What is it, Granger, to be a pessimist? Pessimism is a mental attitude and indeed, the only logical standpoint of mind, given certain postulates.

"When discontent with things as they are takes the form of pessimism, it is indeed a 'divine discontent,' if it embodies the desire to lift mankind from the slough upward and onward to nobler conditions and higher happiness. Such pessimism is justified of her children, and I have never denied my pessimism, or been on bad terms with myself for embracing that attitude.

"I found myself, then, on the horns of an intolerable dilemma. I proved to myself by a thousand secret experiments that I had discovered a panacea for much earthly suffering, and I also convinced myself that, since this discovery was potent for evil as well as good, to proclaim it and make it over to man in his present temper, would endanger the very foundations of society. There was none on earth that I could trust; there is still none on earth that I can trust—Scots caution, perhaps, carried to insane lengths; or else my native idiosyncracy, that ever prompted me to reserve, reticence, suppression. And at this stage my thoughts turned in upon myself, and out of my own character—out of my convictions, even out of my opinions and self-delusion that I was a wise, tolerant and temperate man, there arose the accursed temptation personally to experiment with my newfound energy.

"I resisted the thought, yet could not put it wholly behind me. You will perceive the terrific inducement to right some of the wrongs now crying to heaven; you will remember that I am a man who feels very deeply, that I have a passionate sense of right and wrong, as I see them; that suffering never leaves me unmoved; that I possess a morbid, faulty instinct to take into my own bosom the shafts aimed at mankind in general. These poignant emotions worked havoc with me; and to spare you and the world the narrative of my struggle and the growing sense that if I did nothing, it would soon be too late to do anything, I may relate how there came a time when I determined to take on my own shoulders the garment of my own achievement and not, indeed, proclaim it, but employ it on my own responsibility for the welfare of the world.

"It was the garment of a giant ill-fitted to a dwarf's shoulders, my friend. You may carry the thyrsis, as Plato says. without being possessed by the god. Yet of such fond spirits was I, in my ignorant belief, that because I had discovered the cathartic hurricane, I was also endowed to employ it. There is no man living on this earth endowed to employ it; and no man shall do so!"

He rose and walked up and down the room for the space of five minutes, and I said nothing meanwhile but waited for him to continue. He returned to the fire and presently resumed.

"What spiritually follows I have written, that my generation may appreciate the truth. For the moment, to you, who will be among the last on earth to hear my voice, or look upon me, it remains to detail the physical facts and explain these mysteries. I have used you ill, Granger; but you will forgive me. I have employed you as an unconscious agent to spread untruth and to create false impressions. I have suggested to you monstrous theories, that you might help to disseminate them, hoodwink humanity and hide the secret truth. Deliberately I created this impression and confusion of thought from the outset and deliberately I pretended that I was not out of harmony with the preposterous ideas that a living animal, or living animals, beyond human experience were involved in the extraordinary things that happened. There was, of course, no shadowy grain of truth in any such suggestion. I and I alone am responsible for all that has occurred. I had no agent—human, or super-human. There is no 'Bat'; but the time has now come when you shall understand."

He paused, regarded me fixedly for a moment, and then proceeded.

"Why I did the things that I have done is related in this manuscript; but how I did them I am about to relate, that you may complete the story when I have gone. Follow me now, if you are rested and strong enough to do so."

As we clambered to Sir Bruce's own apartments, I spoke and told him of my adventure on the night before I had left Grimwood during the previous August. He stood halfway up the stairs to listen and did not interrupt me. When I had finished the story, he expressed his deep regret.

"I feel sorry above measure that terrible experience should have overtaken you," he said. "It was a misfortune for which I am in no sense responsible. The explanation of what you saw shall take its proper place in what I am now to tell you."

He opened the door of his private room and locked it after we had passed through. He then turned on the electric light, left a small bedroom and led me into a larger chamber that communicated with it. I found myself in a laboratory, and passing through this, we entered one still larger. Under the bright lamps I saw a bewildering chaos of scientific instruments and machines. The spectacle, though on a far larger scale, reminded me of the workshop of Ian Noble. At one door Sir Bruce stopped and hesitated.

"This chamber contains my raw material," he said, "and though the sight of it would convey no idea to you, yet for your peace of mind I will deny it to you, Granger. You will then be in a position to oppose a blank negative to the battery of questions that will be discharged upon you. My present supply is nearly exhausted, and it is not my wish that any eye shall see it. That the source of my new element will be rediscovered in years to come, none can doubt; and when that time shall arrive, may the world be educated to receive it with reverence, humility and universal love. Only so should man welcome so mighty a boon."

Sir Bruce walked through the scene of his secret labors and made no effort to arrest my progress, or draw my attention to the strange, silent machinery here set up. Once, however, he stopped and spoke.

"It has been a source of grief to my brother, Hugh, that having acquired Grimwood from him, I made no effort to restore it in a manner worthy of so interesting a place. You see the explanation. I never designed to use it otherwise than as a laboratory, wherein secluded I might pursue my scientific work; but I did not know then how invaluable it would become in these great labors. My money has been entirely devoted to my discovery, and my time also. Acquaint the general with these facts. He reinherits Grimwood—the site I mean—for within an hour nothing but the site will remain."

I ventured to beg him to reconsider this determination; but he did not so much as reply.

"Here," he said, gazing about him, "is the theater of my gigantic and futile achievement. Now I will furnish you with details. The place, as you see, was admirably adopted to my needs, and circumstances enabled me to slip into it so naturally that no suspicion has ever attached to my possession. Only three persons have known that my actions were extraordinary, and they have but dimly guessed at them. In any case they were faithful and loyal. They would never have divulged any of my secret movements—my goings and comings, or the manner of them. They are wholly innocent of anything but supreme devotion to me, and the truth was, of course, completely hidden from them. Take pains to make that clear, and see that the terms of my will, in so far as it touches them, are carried out. All three are provided for."

We had reached a shallow flight of wooden steps as he spoke, and in a moment I was standing beside him on the roof of Grimwood. Here, within the battlements and at a point invisible from the ground, stretched a large and level space of asphalt, and at one end was a low shed. It reminded me of the roof at Sir Bruce's bungalow in Chislehurst.

He bade me stand still, then proceeded to the little building and drew from it, as we might bring a horse by its bridle from a stable, "the Bat." By one hand on its neck he led it, and it seemed to glide after him. For a moment the horrible sense that I still faced a living animal possessed me; but I stood firm and swiftly perceived that I confronted nothing but an exquisite engine built in the natural lines of an aerial animal—bird rather than bat.

It was long and spare, created obviously for speed and modeled, as to its exterior, half a brute and half a bird. Sir Bruce touched a lever and the machine's saucer eyes were illuminated; at a touch again it unfurled its great, taut wings.

"The speed is not in them," he explained. "They steer me, no more. This is not an airplane, but a projectile."

He showed me his seat in the body of the creature, and the place of the power, emitted from the region of the vent. It was clear that the engine, or whatever it might be, occupied but little space, and the entire machine, so Sir Bruce informed me, weighed no more than two hundred and fifty pounds.

"It might be much lighter save for the necessity of great speeds," he explained, and then, while I examined the thing, he continued. "Having determined to apply my power to the world's gain, as I believed, there rose the question of how to do so. Were my time to come over again, I should proceed on different lines and start with the assumption that human life is sacred; but the gods seldom give a man a second opportunity. In my original design, the death of enemies to the human race formed the salient feature. It was necessary, therefore, to do two things and employ my energy, not only as a means of destruction for my enemies, but a means of salvation and security for myself. So I built this engine with a double object and speedily found that it would meet every requirement, make me independent of time and space and secure my complete personal safety. It is made of aluminum treated with my new element itself. It has ceased to be aluminum, therefore, and become transmuted to another mineral under the radioactive energy applied to it. Thus you have something even lighter than aluminum and a thousand times more stable. No known amalgam would be able to support the air pressures to which this machine has been subjected. It is impossible to describe them in terms of our knowledge, or suggest the speeds attained. But they are nothing to what greater engines, with increased facilities for outpouring the driving force, might attain."

He showed me the machine from its beak and electrically lighted eyes to the wings—constructed of a metal so thin that it appeared almost translucent. He displayed the tripods, fashioned like huge birds' claws, that supported it and a hundred other minor details all more or less suggestive of a living thing. Apart from its powers, the machine was an extraordinary work of art. He then broke the thread of his explanation and dwelt upon a subordinate point, which interested him more than it interested me.

"We will return a moment to the question of speed, which is closely connected with gravitation. Einstein does not hold gravitation a force, but merely a distortion, or crumpling up, both of time and space before matter. This I have effectively established to be true with the help of my engine. Time ceases to have any significance for me when I am in space, and my element, No. 87 of the Periodic Table, might be so employed that we could create a rate of progress and a range of speeds to take us far beyond our own atmosphere and drive us back into it again if we desired to return. Gravitation, in fact, becomes a word only to be accepted in Einstein's sense.

"I have used but a pinch of my power. I have never taken this thing out of our atmosphere, though tonight I shall do so and for myself annihilate time and space alike. Let me remind you, Granger, of the calculations of M. Esnault-Peltaire, who maintains that a thousand pounds of radium would suffice to carry a man to Venus in thirty-five hours, were such a vehicle as this I have invented available for the journey.

"Have you examined that assertion? If not, I will show you what it means. Venus, at inferior conjunction, which is the period no doubt calculated for, is only twenty-six millions of miles from earth. Save the moon, she is our nearest neighbor in space, and nothing except an occasional comet or meteor has ever approached us so closely. To reach Venus in thirty-five hours, we should need a speed of about seven hundred and forty-three thousand miles an hour; and when I tell you that I have attained to a quarter of that rate of progress, or more than one hundred and eighty thousand miles an hour, in our atmosphere, you will, perhaps, form some idea of what my element means. At such a speed day and night follow upon each other like sunshine and flying cloud shadow. Thus time and space are crumpled, as we take a sheet of paper and tum it into a ball. The wings of the engine are, of course, only used for starting from and descending to earth. When I am moving, the pace would tear them from the hull in an instant. This is, in fact, as I have already told you, not an airplane but a bullet, or rather a rocket, that carries its own propelling force along with it."

He then returned to himself. "I erected this thing for my own security first, and secondly that I might be independent of space and time; I then invented the engine to liberate my energy upon earth, so that I can fertilize a field, or throw down a city at will; and, lastly, I invented the weapon with which I destroy men."

He took something from the inside of the machine and showed it to me by the light of its eyes. It looked like a long, steel knitting needle set in a small pistol handle. But the needle was hollow. He then put some objects a little larger than pins into my hand.

"You may liken this thing to a revolver and these to the cartridges with which I load it," he explained. "These objects contain, first the charge of No. 87 that speeds them on their way at the tremendous pressure necessary to drive so small a thing, and secondly an explosive fragment of the same material in the tiny shell, which operates after the victim has been struck. The difficulty was to correct the charges for both purposes. Experiments on big game in central Africa enabled me to reach the correct values."

He dwelt upon these technical details and also explained the material of the receptacles of the energy, which, like "the Bat," were only created with the help of the energy itself. Without it, I gathered that the power of using it would never have been possible, and here the inventor's difficulties had been enormous, his results extraordinary. He had made a new synthesis of minerals and achieved what were, for practical purposes, new metals with a resisting power beyond all experience.

"Come," he said. "You have now seen what is necessary and can retain the recollection until you have leisure to set it down. We will go back, and I shall tell you how I did what I have done and then read my measured statement—my apologia and farewell."

We descended and he continued his description in detail.

"I knew that Alexander Skeat lived at Queen Anne's Mansions and understood that it was his custom to return home on foot after a lecture, or evening entertainment. I learned his movements therefore, and leaving my bungalow at Chislehurst, where my engine was concealed on the flat roof, descended in St. James's Park a minute later, flung a covering over the machine, which rendered it practically invisible by night, and waited for Skeat, who would almost certainly return home by way of the Suspension Bridge. He came across the park and I shot him at close range. I remembered him well enough and destroyed him instantly. I had only time to return to my vehicle and spread wing before Skeat's cry won a response. I was seen to depart, and my original idea—to build a machine that should resemble a flying animal, and thus confuse human opinion and create an element of fear—proved entirely successful from the first. The animal stench liberated was, of course, a gas manufactured in the laboratory for that purpose.

"The Albert Memorial may be said to have been little more than an experiment. I understood from experts that the mass was worthless as art, and I rained my electrons from above, regulating the discharge with absolute accuracy and convincing myself that the energy could be used with infinite delicacy and exactitude. Indeed I had already done so upon unknown tombs in the central Sahara. My energy is not explosive; it drives downward only thus applied. A watering pot is a clumsy tool by comparison and far less capable of the perfect accuracy I attained before employing the power in cities. On that occasion I left Chislehurst at half past two in the morning, poured my energy a minute later, after attaining perfect equilibrium above the memorial, and returned to my bungalow with the rapidity of light.

"The story of Joseph Ashlar is but a repetition of what I have told you in the case of Skeat. His habits were common knowledge and gave him easily into my hand. Incidentally I was seen again, and again the suggestion of some fabulous animal won ground in the common mind.

"Lorenzo Poglaici's death in midair furnished a scene worthy of a poet's pen. Twice I had flown over the sleeping city of Fiume without adventure and also returned; but on the third night, this picturesque pirate also flew, according to his custom, and I met him and shot him in midair. He attempted to fight and fired his revolver fruitlessly. The mark of a bullet may still be seen upon the body of my machine, but it could not penetrate.

"Of Bronstein, Clos, and Paravicini, it was the second whom I went to Italy to destroy. I concealed my vehicle in the Campagna, took train from a little station to Rome next morning and discovering the lodging of Gerard Clos perceived his route and engaged a couple of rooms in the Piazza di Spagna overlooking it. I shot him and his accomplices in crime from a window at a range of thirty yards, left my apartments on the following day, regained my machine and returned by night. It took me far longer to walk from the little station to the thicket of concealment than to return from Italy to England. In America, I could have destroyed the churches in New York within a minute of the time when Greenleaf Stubbs fell, but to do so by day must have meant the destruction of many innocent beings. I waited for darkness therefore, at an elevation above human sight. From the moment when I finally left New York to the hour I alighted on this roof might have been less than a minute; but again I was delayed by the difference of time and the necessity to return after dark. All that happened in China and Russia is but an echo of what you know.

"Paul Strossmayer and Ian Noble were too easily slain. Concerning that tragedy I will read to you in a moment. From what I have told you, you will understand that it was a very simple matter to destroy them. And when afterwards I heard the truth concerning Noble, I would have given my life a thousand times to undo what I had done. But I erred out of ignorance, not jealousy, alike in murdering the man and destroying his handiwork. He was, as I believed, only Strossmayer's creature, and what I heard from the Jugo-Slav on the night before his death led me to suppose that the secret of No. 87 was already in his hands for terrible purposes.

"As for Owen, last night when you had retired, I went to Chislehurst and left my machine as usual in its hiding place upon my bungalow roof. Later I mixed with the people, stood near

Downing Street at the hour of the minister's departure for the House, and fired through the back of his motor car, using a charge specially prepared for that purpose. I started for Chislehurst after learning that I had not failed, and my intention was to be at Grimwood immediately after dark; but a delay of fog retarded my train on its way back to Chislehurst. The lights you observed burning in my rooms were never extinguished when I left at an early hour this morning. Therefore, on the return of darkness, you observed them."

He stopped weary enough of his own voice; but I could say nothing. I was only concerned to commit to memory all that he had told me.

Presently he spoke again. "I was not aware that you had seen me in the glade the night before you left me, Granger. Perhaps the course of the world's history might have been modified had you summoned courage to challenge me when you returned to the house. After bidding you good night on that occasion, I took my machine out with a view to running a few thousand miles and seeing that all was well. I had not been in the air since my return from America and had encountered heavy weather on the way back. There will be no weather where I am going tonight—a curious thought: no weather. Some trifling fault in the electric lighting caused me to descend a moment after starting. The head of the machine was lowered to mine, that I might adjust it. I rose again, ran for five minutes, sped as far as North Africa, and was probably back in my apartments before you returned to the house. Is there anything else that occurs to you?"

I considered. For a moment I had been overwhelmed by the thought that possibly my cowardice had altered the story of the world's progress. But the immensity of the idea was, perhaps happily, more than my brain could receive. I put the thought from me and one recollection, of ludicrous insignificance, occurred to my mind.

"Had you anything to do with the phenomenal crop of wheat you showed me on one of your farms last August, Sir Bruce?"

He nodded.

"Yes; before the wheat was sown last spring, I trickled the element upon that field, knowing corn was to be planted there. Whether it would blast, or invigorate the crop, I could not tell. It was applied in the most sparing quantities possible. There is no doubt that in this connection radioactivity will produce results upon our foodstuffs impossible to measure without experience."

He rang the bell and Timothy Bassett appeared.

"Are you nearly ready?" he asked.

The old man was cast down and tearful. "Us be most done, master," he said.

"Have no fear for the future, Bassett. And see that the dogs are removed from the kennel when you go. Mr. Granger will summon you shortly. Now bring something to drink; and each of you take a silver memento of me from the dining room. Then remove all the silver and the family portraits to the empty lodge, where you will spend the night." Timothy departed and soon returned with spirits and a siphon.

"My will is with my lawyers," explained Sir Bruce. "My brother will learn that the family possessions, such as they are, have also been deposited with him, save for the things that Bassett will look after. Hugh is a man in ten thousand. The shock of my departure will probably end his days."

He drank and then took his manuscript from the table and read it slowly to me. Life can never parallel that solemn experience.

Chapter XV

Sir Bruce's Narrative

I

"It is a melancholy fact that the flower of human happiness never yet opened without revealing a worm in the bud. Out of new happiness, new sorrow will infallibly be created, and within the heart of the increased prosperity lies hidden an invisible germ, which must presently develop new forces making against happiness. Thus the eternal circle is completed and the tradition of human suffering sustained from generation to generation. Every human advance, every state of melioration, will still bear along with it the inherent defects of its qualities. In their turn the defects are conquered; another advance is won; and from that advance, new trials, problems and sufferings grow, to keep the children of men in a state of everlasting strife against circumstance. For every battle won promises a crop of new foes sprung out of our very triumphs—a new skeleton at our feast of success.

"We walk the stern road of reality but keep our eyes and hopes forever lifted to the unreal, since happiness is no more, at best, than the fitful fire of summer lightning against the darkness of the night in which we move.

"When I discovered the new element, this fact, concerning the truth of happiness, was uppermost in my mind, and before all things I perceived how, from a prodigious, potential blessing, there must arise also the inevitable, new peril hidden in every blessing.

For once the danger was not concealed: 1 perceived it as readily as I perceived the immense access of human happiness to be hoped from No. 87. One had to weigh the one against the other.

"Dean Inge remarks, with that luminous bitterness peculiarly his own, that the fruit of the tree of knowledge always drives man out of some paradise; but my hard-won fruit promised to create a new paradise of this desert we call life—to link the oases in it and turn the dreary antres into smiling gardens. With unspeakable joy I first dwelt on this aspect of my discovery and welcomed its stupendous promise. I believed that Providence had sent my element to make good the void created by the Great War; I pushed forward sleeplessly and it was not until the power to apply and control my radioactive agent had been perfected, that real difficulty and doubt gathered like a fog around me. The application presented problems greater by far than either the discovery, or the control.

"I knew the danger of letting my discovery pass into the hands of middlemen—those parasites bred out of feudal law and corrupt government, which fasten like a tick on the back of all civilized nations. My problem was to apply the energy to universal good purpose; but the machinery for so doing did not exist. Thus the physical difficulties 1 had conquered soon became as nothing before the mightier problem: the means by which my discovery should be launched upon its solemn and salutary task. The creative element was offered—the light waited to irradiate the earth; but man, I found, had as yet no candlestick to hold it. And it is for that reason I extinguish my light again. I have come to the conclusion that the soul of man is not yet sanctified to receive such a bequest; and this I say from no shame and confusion at my own failure—concerning that I have yet to speak—but because now, in these last hours of existence remaining to me, I am still convinced that earth is still unsafe for my discovery.

"Consider the preliminaries of my task. The first thing one connects with an energy is the power to overcome something else. It may be space; it may be an opposed energy; it may be—and in my case with heart and soul I answer that it was—the forces of evil. To overcome evil with my good energy was my dream. But observe how difficulties leapt up before this ambition. I had, to begin with, only my own standards of good and evil; and it was long before I could convince myself that those standards sufficed. In the full strength of my intellect indeed, I repelled any temptation to use my power myself; it was not until the hopelessness of the position had eaten into the very root of my brains, that such an idea entered them. At first I doubted not that my fellow man might be trusted with my discovery. But reflection steadily darkened this opinion, and when I came to particulars, I dared not take any into confidence.

"Where were the minds; where the pure purposes; where the philosophic spirits to be entrusted with my discovery? They did not exist in any State. And still they do not exist. Man continues subject to a thousand shattering inherited instincts; his life is still too much a question of the survival of the strongest; his temptations are too real; his ideals are too base; his ambitions too earthy; his values too gross. He cannot be trusted in the lump; and had better not be trusted at all.

"Certain men and women, indeed, I thought upon, and knew them for noble beings of unstained honor, inspired alone by enthusiasm for humanity and love of truth. But these were not of the world. They lacked knowledge of affairs, or the practical problems that faced me. These fine souls were above and beyond any sense of the sordid proposition that challenged my attention. I had seen the influence of such men and women on executive operations and perceived how, out of the idealistic flowers they offered, came no seed corn to banish the hunger of men. Is it not Montaigne who says that one laughs, not at man's folly, but his wisdom?

"Still therefore I kept silence, although every instinct of the true-born scientific inquirer prompted me to proclaim my discovery; for is not concealment of knowledge the sin against the Holy Ghost—a blow struck at the very spirit of Science itself? Already the world's advance in physics was proceeding by leaps and bounds, leaving religions and ethical progress hopelessly in the rear. The best brains, the rarest intellects were being poured into physics; but, for my own part, I never recognized the divorce between material and spiritual advance; I believed that all right thinking should unite them; and I stood now before the problem of translating No. 87 into terms of the soul! I could not solve that problem; and I knew not where to turn for help in so gigantic a task.

"Now, too late, I see my own aberration and measure the disaster to humanity occasioned by my ultimate resolve, to employ single-handed my own discovery. For in truth nothing can be more vicious and immoral than to suppose that deliberate crime may be employed in any holy cause, or evil done that righteousness shall progress. Out of good, evil indeed may come; but not out of evil, good. For my awful error I am now called to pay the price, and my memory and name, instead of being hallowed by future generations, must ever stand convicted and condemned before the judgment of mankind. That is my penalty and sentence.

II

"I will now traverse the stages of my experiment up to the final and terrible error, which went near to overthrowing my reason and for which no power of atonement exists. It was the culminating folly of an intellect powerful in some directions, weak in others; and the megalomania I have revealed proves once again, if it wanted proof, that no man is strong enough to live to himself; that only along the line of intercommunion, fellowship and social cooperation lies any hope for humanity. I put my trust in myself—one no more fitted to judge and condemn than any other. In fighting the forces of superstition, I was grossly superstitious; in laboring against the might of unreason, I was irrational. I committed all the evils I sought to combat; I used my divine energy exactly as I feared it would be used, if placed in the hands of civilization; I displayed no broad understanding, but a native prejudice and hatred of certain activities and personalities; I proceeded on no philosophic principle, but with the narrow-mindedness, malignity and ignorance of a fanatic and partisan. And I have lived to taste my reward, and see how I advanced, rather than retarded the ambitions of those protagonists I swept out of life; how my tyranny brought fresh followers to their tyrannies, new grist to their accursed mills.

"Woe to me that while I mistrusted all other men, I could not extend that distrust to myself!

"I destroyed Alexander Skeat, holding him a sinister force opposed to national honor and genuine progress. He was an avowed enemy of Science and a scoffer at tradition. What he stood for, rather than himself, called for opposition; but his bad manners, egotism, cynicism and lack of any constructive idea might well have been trusted to efface him and his books in fullness of time.

"After his death, I took part in the subsequent discussions, and myself deliberately contributed to confusion of the issue. The appetite grows by what it feeds upon, and a personal deterioration swiftly developed, taking the shape of unscientific delight in my power and unsocial satisfaction in the possession of my secret. I knew myself unique and felt that the kingdoms of earth would fall down and worship me if I invited them to do so. The disparity between my research and my application must ever form a melancholy subject for psychoanalysis. I held the thunderbolt of Jove and might have rent the round world, or torn a dozen fresh volcanoes in its bosom; I might have swept continents, divided seas, poured fertility upon the hungry lands of the earth; brought manna from heaven; but such was my parochial mind, faulty judgment and failing sense of proportion, that I opened my campaign with no worthier initial effort than the murder of an intellectual conjurer whose activities were sterile, whose fate was of no earthly importance to anybody but himself.

"The Albert Memorial, being worthless on all counts, I employed experimentally. It would have been as easy for me to leave a heap of gold in its place as the transmuted dust they found there; but the playhouse which I subjected to my energy had provoked in me a personal animus. Its entertainment I held inimical to all dramatic progress. I know now that it was in reality harmless and even modest as compared with kindred productions of which I have since heard; but on a personal visit, and from a personal standpoint, I found the play to be animal in its appeal, devoid of any excuse for existence and radically remote in spirit from the land it pretended to represent. That a concoction so barbaric, brainless and sensuous should have delighted London for three years outraged my sense of what a theater ought to be, and I swept it off the earth, leaving, as I supposed, London the cleaner for its destruction. Vain fancy! I have lived to see the same play reproduced with enthusiastic welcome at another house.

"In the case of the great temples of Christian Science, I razed them to the ground, because, in my opinion, there was little warrant for the linking of Christianity with Science, and I found such an association objectionable. It is quite possible that I had not weighed all of the facts, or that I saw these through the eyes of personal prejudice. Be that as it may, I resented violently not only their claims but their methods of advertising them, which seemed to me hardly in keeping with the dignity of a great religion.

"But how has my assault contributed to lessen the growing grip of this cult? Already mightier churches than those I struck down are arising from their dust. Not a man or woman has been weaned from the error; it is more probable that thousands have been won to it as the result of what I accomplished.

"Thus might I retrace, step by step, my operations, only to find the same story repeated with monotonous regularity. Joseph Ashlar is become a saint of Labor, and the anniversary of his destruction may unchain fresh furies, under conditions such as our generation has never known, but will yet suffer. I have lived to see the place destined for Greenleaf Stubbs occupied by one who will chastise with scorpions, where he would have used whips. I have lived to loosen the precious bonds that united England and America, by the murder of that man.

"Lorenzo Poglaici's death served only to hasten an end which the good sense of his nation and the wisdom and patience of Jugo-Slavia must have finally attained, without the destruction of that erratic genius; while not a mad hope, or criminal design cherished by the dead anarchists, Bronstein, Clos, and Paravicini, has departed out of the hearts of their supporters with their assassination. I have heightened rather than dimmed, I have hastened rather than retarded, their red visions of the future.

"Ozama, the Japanese, and that appalling being who has brought Russia to the abyss, came next. The first I slew for his dishonor. He lied to China and prepared to build an infamous conquest on the foundations of falsehood. I had narrowly watched him for three years, and finding no great Power ready, or willing, to intervene on the part of his distracted victim, herself rent in twain, I struck—only to find another of the tribe of Ozama spring into being and carry on the evil work.

"My act in Russia needs no expression of regret. Here the forces of evil did actually concentrate in the brain of one man, and the harvest of my blow at Moscow is already green above the ground.

"But no anarchist in the world's history has ever destroyed a life more precious and rich in promise than have I, when ignorant of truth and fearful that my secret was discovered, I sent Ian Noble out of the world. That awful error crowned my life with a crime as dark as any in the annals of international wickedness. The train by which I reached my mistaken opinions can easily be followed and the vital point occurred at Grimwood during August last, when Ernest Granger offered to tell me of his personal experiences with Noble at our little Club of Friends. Had I listened to what he was anxious to narrate, this story might have ended in a manner very different; had chance brought me into contact with Noble, I should have welcomed his wisdom, perhaps even bestowed upon him as a legacy my knowledge, strong in the consciousness that he would put it to higher purpose than I, and efface the memory of my actions. But chance willed otherwise. I never met him, and I never heard the truth concerning him until he was gone. Instead, through Paul Strossmayer, whom I detested from the moment of our first meeting, I learned that his chemist had discovered the secret of radioactivity and was about to convey it from England to the service of Jugo-Slavia. Upon that information, myself now fallen far from my own sense of justice and ancient judicial faculties, I struck at once, murdered both men and destroyed the lifework of Noble, together with himself. Five nights later I heard the truth of what I had done, and resolved to perish ere my fallen reason committed further crimes against the world. I knew my mind was now disordered and felt that while there remained to me the power to act, I must depart. For my self-control is rapidly passing from me; my intellect is sinking into decay; I am no longer responsible to myself for my actions, as the death of Erskine Owen sufficiently testifies. Nothing save a frantic hatred of his error made me murder him. But shall all men who err pay the price of death for it?

"And now I die, not by the hand of man, but my own. My soul has withered and my humanity shriveled under this scorching test. Only death remains; and my body shall pass to win a tomb in forgiving space; for the dust of which I am formed is unworthy of return to the earth that lent it. I will remove myself from the world forever.

III

"'Nothing requires a rarer intellectualism than willingly to see one's equation written out,' says George Santayana, the wise Spaniard. Such an experience is, however, not new to men of science, and many a servant of truth has been called to face obliteration of his own equation, and see the faithful labors of a lifetime undone as soon as completed. Would that my actions also might be undone along with myself; but they lie in another category than truth and must take their place in time for evermore. To depart needs no courage, for I hunger to do so. That has long been predetermined; but it was only within the last days that I have become fixed to write out the equation of my discovery also, leaving the secret for future generations to re-discover.

"My life and death serve, at least, one purpose and furnish a lesson and a warning for the world. Since Science now lifts her sceptre and ascends into her throne, she must be recognized for the beneficent power to which mankind shall largely look for their contentment, their reconciliation and their happiness. The promised land is a real land, and though my foot may never tread it, my eyes have seen the dawn grow white above its hills and valleys. But before man attains unto it, more than ever grows the necessity to compose his enmities, his jealousies, his rivalries, and practice that renunciation and self-denial, which alone can maintain the spiritual greatness of Kingdoms or breathe life into any League of the Nations. And this I also see: that my fellow creatures must share their world in a larger understanding, a more generous faith, a more international love and compassion ere this, my discovery, can be committed to their charge.

"Before No. 87 is again at the service of mankind, may the earth have sufficiently advanced along the road of reason to make honorable use of it; for that the energy must once more be revealed, if not to our children, then to the generation that follows them, is certain. That those who finally attain the treasure will use it faithfully, we can hope and pray, yet may not affirm.

"This, at least, is certain: there will come a time—it may be soon, it may be late—when man shall achieve the power to mend his earth, or end it; and it is equally sure that not one nation exists today which could be trusted to employ such an energy with a purpose unstained by human greed, or that national selfishness and lust of possession which vitiate so much of promise to mankind. Again and again we stretch out our hands with a welcome for the evangel of glad tidings and good will; again and again our cheers sink to a sigh, as man once more stones his prophets, crushes the weak, and denies his little children the milk of human kindness and the bread of truth."

He finished, rolled up his manuscript and gave it to me without inviting comment.

"And now farewell," he said. "Thank you for what you have done, and what you have yet to do. May life still contain good things for you and afford you such content and peace as you well deserve."

He perceived that I desired to say much and reason with him; but he rose, lifted his hand and indicated that he could not hear me.

Chapter XVI

The Last of Grimwood

It is strange how the idlest detail serves to punctuate a tremendous event, and how memory will often preserve the trifle clean-cut, while mightier matters already grow dim and elude our recollection.

Upon the night of that strange exodus there arises one vision whenever I think of it: the picture of Nancy Bassett weeping and carrying a basket, which contained a mother cat and four kittens.

Sir Bruce summoned his people, when he had taken farewell of me, and bade them "goodbye." They shook his hand and went their way in the extremity of grief. Then I, too, left him and joined my car, where the driver awaited me a quarter of a mile from Grimwood. Bassett, his wife, and daughter had brought their own belongings and such things as Sir Bruce directed—old family pictures and other possessions—to an empty lodge that stood here. But dimly aware of what was to happen, we grouped together in silence waiting for the event.

I knew that Grimwood and all it contained was now to be destroyed, that Sir Bruce would charge his engine to the utmost capacity and then, mounting through earth's atmosphere, perish and pursue his way in his flying tomb whither no man might tell.

It was the dark hour before dawn and one could actually see nothing of what happened; but within twenty minutes we all marked the eyes of "the Bat," like twin sparks of fire, upon the roof of the manor house. The machine ascended and became invisible to us, whereupon through the night there drifted drearily a strange mutter and a moaning—the lamentation, as it seemed, of that ancient Elizabethan pile, shuddering and sinking down under a swift rain of electrons, that transformed the granite at a touch and ground the ancient porphyry into dust.

The dirge of sound persisted for five minutes; then all was silent. I knew what my companions would see in the morning and felt for their sorrow before the destruction of their home; but my own thought followed the destroyer and pictured that personality—so human, and imperfect in itself—now translated to be one of the world's wonders; glorified for its genius and hated for its crimes; rendered egregious, mythic by the manner of its life and death; already perhaps a corpse among the stellar spaces; and lifted for evermore "beyond the arrows, shouts and views of men."

THE END

Also Available